Wolf Games

Granite Lake Wolves, Book 3

True love's path never did run smooth.

After seven years of total denial, Maggie Raynor's body—and her inner wolf—are in full revolt. Weak and shaky, she literally falls into the very large and capable arms of the Granite Lake Beta, Erik Costanov. The last thing she wants is a mate, particularly when just looking at another wolf scares her to death. And one as big and sexy as Erik? Really bad idea, no matter what her libido says.

Erik expected to meet Maggie in Whitehorse to escort her to the home of her sister, his pack's Omega. Sheer chance puts him in the right place at the right time to catch her, but the realization that hits him with the force of a full body shot is no accident. She's his mate. An even bigger shock? She wants no part of him—not until she resolves her issues.

She'll have to work fast, because they're both selected to represent the pack during the premier sporting event for wolves in the north. Not only will she have to work as a team with Erik, she'll have to face down her fear of wolves. Let the Games begin.

Warning: Contains uber-sexy werewolves of Russian descent, reluctant mates and exotic travels through the Yukon wilderness. Includes sarcasm and hot nookie under the Midnight Sun.

Wolf Tracks

Granite Lake Wolves, Book 4

Score one for the underdog...er...wolf.

TJ Lynus is a legend in Granite Lake, both for his easygoing demeanor—and his clumsiness. His carefree acceptance of his lot vanishes, though, when his position as best man brings him face to face with someone he didn't expect. His mate. His very *human* mate. Suddenly, one thing is crystal clear: if he intends to claim her, his usual laid-back attitude isn't going to cut it.

After fulfilling her maid-of-honor duties, Pam Quinn has just enough time for a Yukon wilderness trip before returning south. The instant attraction between her and TJ tempts her to indulge in some Northern Delight, but when he drops the F-bomb—"forever"—she has second thoughts. In her world, true love is a fairytale that seldom, if ever, comes true.

Okay, so maybe staging a kidnapping wasn't TJ's *best* idea, but at least Pam has the good humor to agree to his deal. He'll give her all the northern exposure she can stand—and she won't break his kneecaps.

Now to convince her that fairytales can remake her world—and that forever is worth fighting for.

By popular demand: Clumsy sidekick wolf grows up, sarcasm reigns, and the wilderness gets wilder. Includes hot nookie in places you expect—like a remote cabin—and places you don't.

Look for these titles by
Vivian Arend

Now Available:

Under the Midnight Sun

Vivian Arend

Samhain Publishing, Ltd.
11821 Mason Montgomery Road, 4B
Cincinnati, OH 45249
www.samhainpublishing.com

Under the Midnight Sun
Print ISBN: 978-1-60928-286-8
Wolf Games Copyright © 2011 by Vivian Arend
Wolf Tracks Copyright © 2011 by Vivian Arend

Editing by Anne Scott
Cover by Angie Waters

Wolf Games, ISBN 978-1-60504-968-7
First Samhain Publishing, Ltd. electronic publication: March 2010
Wolf Tracks, ISBN 978-1-60928-233-2
First Samhain Publishing, Ltd. electronic publication: October 2010
First Samhain Publishing, Ltd. print publication: October 2011

Contents

Wolf Games

Dedication

To Valerie Tibbs, the first reader of the Granite Lake Wolves, and the first to tell me I was a real writer. You're a wonderful friend, a great encourager and a talented graphic artist to boot. Thanks for believing in me.

Anne—you're incredible. We've tagged you The Queen of the Wolves for a reason. Thanks for making the wolfies shine so bright.

To my hubby. Any place we go together is home.

Chapter One

Maggie hesitated as the boardwalk underfoot blurred.

"You okay?"

She nodded but grabbed another couple of pills from her backpack and chased them down with a few swallows of water. Her dizzy spells had grown more frequent. Was she really okay? Not yet, but the cure might be closer than before.

"You're seriously freaking me out. If I didn't know better I'd suspect you were popping something other than herbal remedies." Pam blocked her path and looked her over sternly. Finally seeming satisfied, her friend grabbed Maggie's gym bag off her shoulder. "Since you insist you need to soak instead of just hitting the sleeping bags, I'm going to be your Sherpa. You concentrate on walking. I don't want to have to figure out how to carry your sorry ass again."

Maggie chuckled faintly. "Hey, it only happened one time."

"Yeah, once was enough. You may look like a twig, but you're damn heavy." Pam winked, then offered her elbow. "Do you need an extra hand? I'm here for you."

"I'm fine. Really. I just need a couple hours floating. Liard Hot Springs is a little bit of heaven on earth."

They walked in companionable silence down the worn boards of the four-foot-wide path leading into the bush of northern British Columbia, summertime heat rising around them. Beautiful weather had followed them the entire trip from Vancouver. The bright green colours of new growth in the marsh grasses on either side of the boardwalk made a soul-refreshing break from the concrete that had filled Maggie's world for far too long. Towering spruce trees, the brilliant blue of the June sky, crisp clean air—all of it slipped into her blood like a tonic. A tightly locked knot in her core loosened, and for the first time in almost a decade she didn't resist.

Her wolf stirred.

Oh God, that felt amazing. Maggie stopped in midstride and closed her eyes to let the sensation roll over her. Surround her. Like an icy cold barrier had broken open a crack, shivers trickled through her limbs. Electric. Delightful.

"Shit, are you having a seizure or something?" Pam clutched her arm and shook her gently. Maggie fought to keep from baring her teeth. Because wouldn't that just freak the human out to learn there were some secrets even best friends didn't share.

They were close to the changing shelters, rustic wooden squares built of upright rough-cut timber. Splashing noises trickled to Maggie's ears as she fought down the longing in her limbs she refused to answer. "I'm just tired. Let me get into the water."

"Fuck that. You have...drown. Just...careful...hell." Pam's voice faded in and out of Maggie's range of hearing. It was the most confusing thing. Maggie saw her friend's lips continue to move, but the words disappeared. All that remained was this loud buzzing noise, like a swarm of horseflies. Maggie tried not to laugh at the funny expression on Pam's face as she waved her arms frantically and flapped her hands at someone racing around the corner of the decking surrounding the hot springs.

Someone? Maggie peered harder through the fog drifting in front of her eyes. That wasn't a person, it was a walking wall. Crap, the man was huge. Dripping wet from head to toe, gorgeous tattoos seemed to writhe on his torso as he reached for her.

Hmm...he smelt delicious.

Strength.

Safety.

Sensations of happiness and contentment stole through her chaotic thoughts. Her feet didn't seem to be touching the ground anymore, and the world bounced gently. She cracked open one eye to gaze around. Above her, the trees rotated, and a small cloud chased across the sky in a blur. Warmth surrounded her up to her neck and she let out a contented sign. Her head rested on something firm and soft and she nuzzled against it tighter. A steady banging echoed in her ear, somehow reassuring.

And that scent? *Oh yeah.* She drew a deep breath, filling her nostrils and enjoying the way her mouth watered. It was like sitting down to a well-cooked rib-eye steak, with all her favorite side dishes. The sweetest dessert, followed by a dozen shooters. Maggie took another leisurely inhalation before snuggling closer to the thumping noise.

Erik caught sight of the women as they strolled down the boardwalk, one of them swaying from side to side. He laughed quietly. He'd have a set of slightly tipsy females to keep an eye on while they soaked. The youth from his pack traveling with him played off to the left in the cold pool section of the natural hot springs. Splashing and hooting and the sounds of carrying-on filled the air.

Wolves—they were such children.

He waded through the water toward the deck. The woman on the right looked familiar. Petite, blonde, youthful features. If she'd been hugely pregnant he would have sworn it was Missy, the Omega for his pack, although she wasn't the kind to get falling-down drunk. It appeared he was about to meet his reason for driving south sooner than expected. It had to be Maggie weaving toward him.

He watched with growing concern as the women's forward motion slowed. It wasn't just a tipsy ramble anymore, something seemed wrong. Erik grabbed the edge of the railing, wondering if he should offer assistance.

"Oh shit, help, someone. Damn it. Help." The brunette waved her arms, the frantic motions drawing his attention to the other woman as she wavered on unsteady limbs. He leapt out of the water, droplets spraying from his body to soak the worn boards underfoot. Long strides carried him down the boardwalk just in time to be able to catch the blonde before she collapsed.

His world shifted three feet to the left.

Shocks—like small electrical connections—registered where their bodies touched. Trickles shot through his limbs and up his spine. Tingling. Snapping. *Oh hello*, it felt completely and wonderfully right.

"Thanks—she's been getting dizzy and I didn't want her to collapse and hurt herself." The dark-haired woman kept rambling, but the entire focus of Erik's attention centered on the beautiful female he held in his arms. He turned and walked back to the water, taking the steps while still cradling her close.

"What the hell are you doing? She's passed out. She needs to recover and—" The friend followed him down into the pool, tugging at his elbow.

"—stay warm. Don't worry, I've got her." Erik had no

intention of letting her go. Ever. But that probably wasn't what this other woman wanted to hear. He settled on one of the submerged benches scattered through the natural pool and rearranged his mate in his arms, her head resting on his chest. The sensation of her cheek on his bare skin made his whole body react.

His mate.

Incredible. After all these years of waiting and longing, she dropped into his arms out of the blue. For now, knowing she actually existed was enough to make him want to shout in delight. Except, he didn't do shouting.

A rather piercing voice broke through his intense concentration and he remembered the friend, now glaring at him with suspicion. He held out his free hand. "Erik Costanov, from Alaska."

The brunette ignored his hand. "Pam. I think you should let me take care of my friend now."

"I've got her."

"I noticed. I'd prefer it if you weren't holding her. Just take her over to the stairs and I'll help—"

"Relax. I won't hurt her." *I'm going to care for her for the rest of my life.* The thought sent shots of pleasure through his system. Finally. His mate.

"Really, I'm not comfortable—"

"She's comfortable." It was true. The small armful of blonde snuggled in tighter and Erik's heart swelled. Hmm. This was going to be wonderful. Except for the fainting bit. They'd have to figure out what was causing it and—

A splash of water struck him in the face. "Hey, buddy. Thanks for stopping Maggie from hitting the deck, but I'll take over now. Got it?" Pam tugged on his arm, causing small waves to splash everywhere.

Erik took a deep breath. Maggie. He'd been right. He laughed at the irony. All this time waiting and his mate was the sister of his Omega. Why hadn't he known?

"Look, mister, I don't know what the hell you think is so funny—"

A soft groan rose from Maggie. "Pam, can you stop the shouting for a sec? You're killing me here." *Oh hell, even her voice made his body sing.* She squirmed and he carefully cradled her against him, keeping her head above water.

Pam leaned over and looked her in the eye. "Maggie? Can you hear me?"

"Are you kidding? They heard you in Vancouver. Stop screaming, my head hurts enough already. If you want to be helpful, I'm thirsty."

"There's a bottle of water in my backpack. Pass her to me and go get it," Pam demanded, giving him the evil eye.

Bossy chick. Erik smiled. It was good to know his mate had a friend who wanted to protect her, although he would provide all the protection needed from here on out. Conveniently, the teens traveling with him had gathered close, curious to see what was happening.

"Cody, grab some water for our friends," he ordered. The boy nodded and raced for their cooler on the deck.

Maggie wiggled again and Erik savoured the weight of her on his lap. The brush of her skin against his increased his pleasure. The sweet smell of her natural perfume filled him with the dire need to taste her skin.

Cody handed over a bottle of water and she guzzled most of it down.

Pam watched him like an overeager chaperone, her gaze

dancing around the pool area. She seemed concerned there were now four strange males crowding her and Maggie, and Erik motioned for the boys to step away.

"Did I pass out?" Maggie spoke soft and slow, her words barely audible.

"You weren't out cold, but neither were you were coherent. Do you need your pills?" Pam asked.

Maggie leaned back on his chest, her head turned slightly so the warmth of her breath brushed him. "No pills. This is heavenly. I haven't been this relaxed for months."

Erik smiled. She knew him too. Her body already sensed they were meant to be together.

The friend glared harder, her eyes narrowing in suspicion as if Erik were somehow making Maggie respond like a puppet. "Umm, Mags? If you're feeling up to it, you want to come sit over here with me?"

"Nope. Comfy here." Her words slurred.

He peered over the top of her head to see her eyes were closed. Long dark lashes rested on milky white skin. He admired the contrast against his darker colouring where her arm rested on his biceps. She draped herself over him without shame, accidentally grinding her hips against his groin and his cock woke. *Oh yeah.* Getting to the intimate part of their relationship would be fine as well.

She moved lazily, lifting her arms to stretch. Her fingers missed brushing his cheek by inches and he refrained from leaning closer to let her stroke him. Her wonderful scent lingered in the air and he inhaled deeply in appreciation. *Hmm.* All those days of watching his Alpha pair care for each other brought his anticipation for this moment to a fine peak. So this is what it felt like to find the missing part of your soul.

Maggie smacked her lips. "Is there a snack bar here?"

"Are you hungry?" Pam hovered closer.

"No. Just trying to figure out what that fabulous smell is. Why were you shouting?"

Pam pointed over Maggie's shoulder and sniffed. "He is being stubborn and I really wish you'd stop sitting on him."

The steady beat of his mate's heart sped up. She reached under the water and her fingers slipped over the bare skin of his thigh, sending another thrill along his nerves. Oh hell yeah, the connection rocked between them.

"Pam? Where am I?" Maggie twisted in slow motion to stare up at him, the deep blue of her eyes flashing with recognition for an instant before she opened her mouth.

And screamed.

Chapter Two

Maggie scrambled off his lap so fast she slipped, her feet skidding on the soft rocks at the bottom of the outdoor pool. The towering mass of man in front of her caught her easily before her head went under.

"Take it easy, Maggie. You're safe." He settled her on her feet and stepped back. The bright smile in his eyes and on his face made something inside her twist and leap for joy at the same time. Her wolf fought to be free and her stomach clenched in reaction.

He was a werewolf. She recognized him from pictures Missy had sent online over the past couple of years. He was the damn Beta for her sister's pack and he was here in Liard Hot Springs pool and her wolf lusted for him. *Great. Let's just jump in with two feet, shall we?* After avoiding everything to do with wolves for years, the first one she met had to turn her crank. Movement to his side caught her attention as a group of young men approached.

"Erik? Is that Maggie?"

"Of course she is. She looks like her sister. Hi, Maggie, welcome to the North."

The three youths continued to advance, all talking at once. Maggie backed up rapidly, slamming into Pam's side. Oh God, there were four wolves in front of her. Panic rose and she pushed it down. She had to get over her fears.

"Do you know these people?" Pam wrapped a protective arm around her shoulders.

Erik nodded. "We're friends of her sister. We were supposed to meet you in Whitehorse."

Pam looked around pointedly.

One of the boys spoke up. "We begged Erik to bring us to the hot springs. It's been a while and with the Games starting soon and us not being able to participate yet he—"

"Games?"

Erik broke in, his gaze locked on Maggie. She kept eye contact only through sheer will power. "We were supposed to meet tomorrow. It's just a lucky break we're here at the same time. Are you okay now, Maggie? Do you need me for anything?" The heat in his eyes let her know his offer was wide open to interpretation.

Strip and let me ride you. Maggie felt her skin flush, and it wasn't from the heat of the water around them. Was this really happening to her? She shook her head and finally noticed she still wore her shorts and T-shirt over her swimsuit. "Let me get changed and then we can talk."

Pam held her elbow and together the two of them slogged their way out of the pool to the change house, a trail of water following them. Maggie snickered as she glanced at her friend.

"Sorry for making you take a swim with all your clothes on."

Pam waved a hand. "Forget it. You feeling better?"

"Yeah. I think I'll be okay now."

"Good." Pam pulled off her shirt and wrung it out. She peeked out the door of the change shelter and snuck back to whisper. "Are these guys safe? Do you really know them?"

Maggie sat on the bench to wrestle her wet runners off her feet. "I know *of* them. I've never met them but my sister did say someone would come escort me from Whitehorse to Haines. She didn't want me driving by myself after I drop you off at the airport."

"She couldn't come? At least so you'd know they were who they say they are?"

Maggie snorted. "From the sounds of it, Missy doesn't fit in a car very well right now. The soon-to-arrive twins are making her life difficult and I certainly don't expect a pregnant woman to sit for a four-hour trip just to make me feel better. Don't worry, I recognize Erik. He works with my brother-in-law's family. He's a wilderness guide."

"He's a tank."

A burst of laughter escaped her. "He is rather large, isn't he? Rather...yummy, too."

Pam raised her eyebrows. "Really? Crap, Mags, I haven't seen you express interest in anything male for..." She stopped and frowned. "Have I ever seen you express interest in a guy?"

Maggie hit her. "Stop it."

"If he's someone you trust, fine. I just think it's weird that of all places to meet, it's out here in the wilderness. I thought the North was this vast wild land, with wild creatures running free everywhere. Not a social club."

They stepped out of the change shelter and Maggie took a deep breath as the three young men did cannonballs into the lower pool, chasing each other like puppies. "Oh, I think there's plenty of wild animals around, if you know where to look."

Erik watched contently as the youths finally lured Pam to another section of the pool to play a game, leaving him alone with Maggie for the first time. She sat on the narrow edge of grass at the side of the pool, dangling her feet in the water. The thick underbrush of the wilderness behind her framed her sweet body. She clutched the mossy surface with her fingers, head averted, but he knew she was looking him over.

He stood from where he'd sat, neck deep in the hottest part of the pool. Slow, even steps brought him closer until he leaned his elbows on the grass at her side. He breathed in deeply and noticed she did the same, a fluttering pulse leaping to life at the junction of her neck and shoulder. Turning his head he admired her openly, unable to tear his gaze away. She wore a bikini of brilliant blue that matched her eyes, like a little bit of the summer sky had fallen to earth. Her curves and dips and rounded places all called to him and he swallowed hard.

Her head lifted and their gazes met. A trace of fear shone in the depths and his wolf poked him in the nuts, insistent he take care of her.

"Do I frighten you?"

She licked her lips, leaving them wet and soft. He wanted to lean over to taste her so badly.

"I'm very drawn to you, and that scares me."

The air around them filled with the faint noises of the spring and the laughter of the others in the distance. The sunlight shone full on them and she turned her face to its warmth. He waited patiently. Patience was something he had more than enough of. It took a few minutes before she sat straighter, squaring her shoulders. The boldness with which she turned to face him made him proud. His mate was no wimp. He'd expect her to be as strong as him.

"I don't know how much my sister told you. I've been avoiding wolves for a long time. I know I need to change my reaction, but it's become a habit to stay away from any involvement with pack. I have to fight my first instinct. It's going to take time to retrain myself not to panic when I see a werewolf. I'm sorry I screamed when I saw you. You didn't deserve that."

She was not only strong, she was empathetic and caring. Erik let the pleasure of her presence roll over him. "Trust me, you're not the first person to scream at the sight of me. I'm a little larger than most people. That can be intimidating. I don't take it personally."

Maggie smiled. "Good for you."

They stared at each other.

"Would you be comfortable if I touched you?" she whispered, looking him straight in the eyes.

Comfortable? He was dying for her touch. "I'd love it."

She lowered her gaze again. "I haven't been around many wolves recently. I'm frightened by what I'm feeling. I think I know what this is, but I'm scared..."

Oh mercy. "I'll take care of you."

He took a step to the side, still standing waist deep in the water. With one hand on the grass on either side of her hips he caged her between his arms. They both glanced toward the others to make sure they weren't being watched. Then like conspirators, they leaned together and their lips connected.

Sweet summertime air. The feel of the wind through his fur on a moonlight run. All the most treasured moments of his life faded in comparison as he tasted her. This, this was the moment he'd waited for all his life. She met him with her mouth slightly open, her breath mingling with his before their tongues even touched. He forced himself to keep his hands in place but she had no such compunction. As they kissed, slow and easy, learning each other's flavour, she caressed his shoulders, rubbing her palms over his brush cut. Smoothing her long

25

fingers down his chest. His skin shivered in anticipation of where she would touch next. Light, fleeting touches that brought his blood to a boil.

He concentrated on enjoying her scent, drawing it into his very being. Nibbles on her bottom lip, light kisses across her cheek. He licked softly at the pounding pulse at her throat. His gums itched with the desire to bite, to mark her permanently as his. But not yet. Not now that she'd confessed her fears. Still, his wolf demanded he take some action. The beast within grew as wild as he'd ever felt it, driving Erik to claim his mate. Instead of biting he suckled, drawing the soft skin of her neck into his mouth until he'd brought the blood to stain the creamy surface. The moan of desire escaping her lips nearly made him change his mind and take her right there on the embankment.

Oh hell, he wanted her. All his. Now.

It took concentration to pull away, to watch her panting breaths slowly calm, his body aching for more. His gaze fell on the rosy circle marring her throat and his wolf grumbled with delight. *His mate.* He paused.

"Your friend is full human, isn't she?"

Maggie ran her hands over his shoulders again and again, her fingers clinging to him. She peeked at where Pam still played with the boys. "There's no way I can explain to her why I'd let a total stranger give me a hickey. She's going to think I've gone insane." She snorted. "Maybe I have. Oh Lord, I never expected this to happen."

Erik lifted her off the edge and lowered her into the water. He longed to pull her back onto his lap, and touch her more and more intimately. If this had been any normal situation, they would already be making love. It was the way with mates. Sometimes it took a lifetime to find the one special person who would complete you on every level—physical, mental and emotional. Once you found each other there was no hesitation. No recrimination for simply taking and joining together what was meant to be.

Waiting was going to kick his ass.

He took a seat on one of the underwater benches opposite her. "We don't have to tell her. She's flying back to Vancouver in a couple of days, right?"

Maggie nodded.

"We'll wait. As much as I want to take you back to my tent and make love with you right now, we can wait for the sake of your friend." A shiver shook Maggie briefly and she glanced at him, a trace of fear back in her eyes. His wolf howled and fought to comfort her. "What's wrong?"

"I don't want a mate."

He snorted. *Bullshit.* "Too bad. You've got one."

Her jaw dropped, and she gaped at him. "You can't just say something like that and expect me to be all right with it. I'm telling you I don't want a mate. I'm still freaked out at the thought of trying to live within the confines of a pack. Why would I also want a mate to deal with?"

That made no sense at all. "A mate isn't to deal with, a mate is to love."

She stopped cold. He had the sudden vision of the two of them, tangled together intimately, and had to reach into the water to adjust himself before his cock exploded. Her gaze followed his hands and she blushed hard.

"I know this isn't fair. I'm sorry, I really am, but as much as my body is interested, we can't do this. I'm telling you straight up so you can be prepared. Even after Pam leaves, I'm not having sex with you. I'm not ready to be anyone's mate until I deal with some issues."

"Are you telling me this because you think if you say it, you'll be able to resist wanting to be with me? Maggie, we're werewolves and we're mates. There's a chemical reaction between us, yes, but this isn't just physical. Becoming mates is in our best interest."

"Best interest? What the hell are you talking about?"

"Those issues you mentioned, let me help you with them. That's my job. As mates we're better as a couple. I need you, you need me."

"Arghh, you are so frustrating."

"I'm your mate."

The shouting and laughter from the others got louder as they moved closer. This conversation would have to be put on hold. Erik raised a brow at her. "We'll have to agree to disagree for now. Let's head back to the campground. We'll follow you to Whitehorse in the morning. Keil gave me orders to keep you in sight at all times while we're there." He stood and held out a hand to her. She took it reluctantly and he squeezed her fingers. "It's going to be okay, Maggie, really."

She shook her head. "You just don't understand."

They waded to the stairs and he led her out of the pool. "Maybe not, but that doesn't mean I don't care."

The bright hope in her eyes calmed his fears. There was obviously something big she wasn't sharing yet, but they'd deal with it. Together.

"Holy cow, what happened to your neck?" Pam exclaimed as she and the boys crowded around them.

Maggie froze for a second, her face flushing red. Erik stepped in smoothly. "Bug bite."

One of the boys snorted and Erik elbowed him in the ribs while Pam dug into her bag and pulled out a container of cream. She dabbed some on the mark. "Must have been a hell of a big bug."

Maggie glared at him and he smiled, turning away to head to the change room. "The biggest around."

Chapter Three

"I've changed my mind about heading home. I'm canceling my flight, Maggie. I'm not letting you head off into the wilds of Alaska with this group of misfits." Pam folded her arms in front of her.

Maggie sighed. *Not again.* The entire seven-hour drive from Liard to Whitehorse, Maggie had struggled to answer her friend's endless nosy questions. It didn't help that during their couple days of sightseeing in Whitehorse before Pam's fight home, Erik shadowed them everywhere. He seemed to be trying his best to give them a little space but still refused to leave her alone.

"I'm not headed into the wild with them. I'm simply getting a ride to Haines to rejoin my family."

"Yeah, right. The family you've been soooo thrilled about. It's been years since your parents' accident. I thought you told me your sister was involved in some kind of a cult at one point. You never wanted anything to do with her friends when we were at university. There was that one time you even hid from them. Or don't you remember?"

A shiver ran over her skin at the memory. She wished she could forget. "Damn it, Pam. Of course I remember, but things have changed."

"Right."

Maggie hesitated. How was she supposed to convince Pam when she wasn't sure herself? A wolf pack was supposed to be the safest place on earth. A place to be nurtured and cared for, not a hellish trap. That hadn't been her sister's experience, or her own. In defense, she'd rejected the pack of her youth, had even managed to reject the whole idea of being a wolf for a long period of her life. She couldn't do it anymore. Her body wouldn't let her.

But her heart and mind were terrified to take the next step.

She settled into one of the rigid plastic chairs in the airport waiting area. "Pam, I know it seems strange, but you've got to trust me on this. My sister and I have always kept in touch and I love her dearly. Plus she's married to a wonderful guy now."

Pam shook her head reluctantly. "I just don't understand why after all this time you're deciding to move back to the Yukon. I thought we were going to keep rooming together. I'm...disappointed." She squatted beside Maggie. "I'm worried about your health. You've never shaken off this mono or whatever it is you've got. What if you have another attack while you're on the road?"

"That's part of the reason I won't be driving." She grabbed Pam's hands. "I'm going to be fine. Really. I'm so glad we got to spend this time together. You kick butt when it comes to singing on road trips." Pam snorted and they grinned at each other.

"I couldn't sing my way out of a paper bag." Suddenly Maggie was wrapped in a huge hug, the breath squeezed from her body. Pam let her go only to shake a finger in her face. "I want regular emails. Let me know when you're settled and if I don't hear from you often, I'm coming back with a gun."

Maggie laughed. "I expect you to visit me in Haines when you can. You've been an awesome friend. I'm going to miss

31

you."

One last final hug and Pam joined the short line winding its way through the security checkpoint. Maggie felt him at her side before she saw him. While it freaked her out a little to have Erik hovering over her, it also felt very right. The two days she'd shopped and visited the theater and museums with Pam, his presence in the background had reassured her. Made her feel safe. No wonder Pam thought she was crazy to go anywhere with him—he was like an obsessed stalker in her friend's eyes. Now through final security, Pam turned back to wave farewell. She gave Erik a dirty look and held her fingers like a phone, pointing at Maggie and mouthing "call me".

Maggie would miss her, but dealing with the pack for the first time in years with a human around? Not a good idea.

"She's a nice girl." The deep timbre of his voice hit her low in the gut. "You okay?"

She nodded. The familiar protective layers she'd built around her for years were disappearing fast. Now she headed into dangerous territory. Oh damn, was it possible to get comfortable being around a huge group of wolves again? Would she ever feel safe?

"I left the boys at the Canada Games Center to play for a while. I'd like to take my mate out for lunch." He slipped an arm around her, tugging her to his side.

A thrill shot through her at the layers of meaning she could read into his words. His claim on her—she couldn't deny it was real. Her wolf pranced at the thought of going anywhere with him. Especially somewhere private where they could remove a few articles of clothing and get intimate.

She shook her head to break free of the images taunting her. She couldn't. They shouldn't. Not...yet. "I told you we're waiting. I meant it."

He twisted to face her, their bodies sliding closer. "You think it's too dangerous to share lunch with me?" Heat rolled off his skin and she had to look way, way up to see into his eyes. Her mouth watered, her hormones kicking into high gear.

Bastard. He knew how much his touch affected her. "You're a royal pain in the ass."

"Not yet." He stroked her hip intimately, cupping her butt cheek in one palm briefly. He winked, then pressed his wide hand on her lower back to direct her steps toward the parking lot. Heat shot through her core, and her wolf sat up and begged. Maggie jerked free from his touch by picking up the tempo. Of course, since her legs were much shorter, she almost had to run to outpace him. She twirled and planted her hands on her hips. She needed to regroup before they headed to Haines.

"Look. I know you've got direct orders from your chief Pooh-Bah, but I'd like some time by myself. No one is going to accost me on the streets of Whitehorse. I'm perfectly safe. I used to live here. I just want to be left alone and..."

Lordy, how was she supposed to stay angry with him when every time she gave him hell, he did nothing but smile? It wasn't just any kind of smile, it was a do-you-want-to-crawl-into-bed-with-me-now kind of smile. The expression had a lot of impact when you placed it on his six-foot-five frame and added in his gorgeous features and his dark sparkling eyes.

Did he have to smell so damn good?

"You can't walk by yourself in Whitehorse. I don't know if you noticed over the past couple days, but there are a lot more wolves living here than in Vancouver. Not only are you a member of a rival pack, you're also related to a couple of the most powerful wolves in the North. Keil thought you were single. He didn't want any young pups trying to take advantage of you."

"I am single."

He growled softly and her core muscles tightened in reaction. Oh shit, she'd pissed off his wolf. Icy fingers of dread raced up her spine and her heart pounded. She wanted to drop to her knees and bare her throat in submission. Another part wanted to scramble away, to flee from his anger. Somehow she kept her eyes open in the hopes she'd be able to duck if he swung at her. With his height advantage, he towered over her, and she felt overwhelmed by the sheer size of the man.

He lifted her chin with a single finger and spoke firmly. "You. Have. A. Mate." Her wolf panted in agreement and crawled closer to the surface. She grabbed her stomach as cramping pain rocked her. "Damn it, what the hell...?" Erik wrapped his arms around her, pulling her close. Somehow she ended up in his lap as he squatted on his heels, his back against a rental car. The world spun in circles and she scrambled for the vial of pills in her pocket. He took it from her, shook out a few and handed them over. From somewhere he produced a water bottle and she gulped greedily. She kept her gaze averted. Between her fears and her rising need for him, she felt completely out of balance.

It didn't take long for the pain to ease. When she opened her eyes it was to stare into his concerned face.

"I'm so sorry. I didn't mean to scare you." He cupped her face in his big palm, examining her carefully.

She nodded slowly. All she sensed was his concern and desire. She ignored her tangled nerves and forced herself to calm down. He'd been nothing but trustworthy, and he deserved to be treated with respect.

"You want to tell me what's wrong?"

Maggie bit her lip. "Chemical imbalance." For now, that's all she wanted to admit.

He frowned. "You're a wolf. Change and you'll heal."

She scrambled off his lap and wavered for a second before his strong arm supported her. That was one topic she was nowhere ready to discuss with him. "I'm hungry. Can we have lunch?"

Erik eyed her as he led her to his SUV. "Nice try at changing the topic. Why are you fighting this so hard? You need—"

"I need lunch. Something raw. Is that possible here in Whitehorse?"

His smiled wryly. "I know just the place."

"A combo platter for four please."

Maggie elbowed him. "Four?"

Erik sniffed. She must be extra hungry, maybe that was part of her problem. Silly women were always on diets when they didn't need to be. "Sorry, make it for six. Everything raw, extra wasabi on the side, and skip the pickled ginger." They grabbed spots at the end of the long counter and he held her high-backed stool as she sat, still chuckling.

"You turkey. That's not what I meant."

"What?" He captured her hand in his and held it. She might want to go slow but there was no way he would let her completely ignore the fact they were meant to be together. He wanted to touch her, just to torment himself. A flush covered her cheeks and she tugged slightly, testing his hold, before relaxing and squeezing his fingers.

"I'm sorry. I'm not making this easy for you." Her smile faded, and he hurried to reassure her.

"Trust me, I've seen mated pairs in action often enough to know their relationships are not always easy. I'm prepared for anything you send my way." He brushed the fingers of his free hand against her cheek. "I'm all yours."

The light chatter of tourists carried around them, the scents of people filled the air, but all he noticed was her. Bright blue eyes stared at him. The teasing light fragrance of her perfume, the stronger scent of her wolf—both filled his nostrils and clouded his mind.

His stomach rumbled and broke the intense connection between them. Concern for her health nagged at him. There was something wrong with his mate, and he struggled to understand. Wanted to fix things and make her better. He needed more details. "You want to tell me what the pills are about?"

She wrinkled her nose. For a second he thought she might try to lie, but then she sighed. "I've got some kind of chemical imbalance, and I discovered by chance the pills help change my blood pH enough to knock me back to normal levels for a while."

"I still don't see why your wolf doesn't heal you. Does Missy know about this?"

She nodded slowly.

That was good enough for now. For the past two years Missy had often shared her concern for her sister, how she felt Maggie needed to be back with family as soon as possible. He'd have more time to talk about the situation when they were safely on pack land.

"I'll trust she'll do what she can to help you. You let me know if I can do anything, okay?" Erik kissed her cheek lightly, using the opportunity to suck in a deep breath of her scent. Hell. This was sheer hell.

The area grew more crowded. Their tray of food arrived, distracting him for a second. Maggie stopped chatting, closing in on herself. Erik glanced around to see other wolves had joined them and now sat at the counter.

One slid closer to Maggie and leered. "Hey, sweet thing. You new in town?"

Erik lifted a brow. Was the man an idiot? Or blind?

It wasn't even worth making a commotion. Wordlessly, he transferred Maggie from her stool to his lap. He selected a piece of sushi and lifted it to her lips. "Ignore him. You said you were hungry. Try this."

She shot him a grateful look and snuggled closer. "Thank you, although you need to stop hauling me around like I'm a sack of potatoes."

She accepted the tidbit and her tongue stroked his skin. He clenched his jaw hard to stop from growling out loud. That's how she wanted to play it? Okay by him. Anything to keep touching her.

They might have been alone. The new wolves left quickly after realizing he and Maggie were together, and for the first time in a long while, Erik was glad his sheer size was enough to intimidate. Seated at the end of the restaurant counter, his back to the wall, Erik fed piece after piece of delicate salmon, fresh tuna and other sashimi to his mate. After the first couple of times Maggie shyly picked a portion and offered it to him in return.

He sucked her fingers into his mouth, licking them clean one by one, his gaze never wavering from hers.

She whimpered, soft and low in her throat, and he had to close his eyes to concentrate on keeping his wolf at bay. Everything about the woman called to him, but she seemed to be going out of her way to drive him wild. She was strong, but needed his protection. Smart, yet tender hearted. He drew her close and kissed her briefly, brushing their lips together. His hand skimmed over her thigh, tugging her closer into his lap and against his rising erection.

She had to know he wanted her.

Maggie licked her lips, then returned to feeding him. It was as erotic as they could get in a public place. It was a good thing they *were* in a public place, or he'd never have lasted. A few of the barriers she'd raised between them seemed to have slipped away. He glanced at his watch. There was just enough time to finish their meal, pick up the boys and be on their way.

He chose another piece and held it to her lips. He was going to enjoy every possible moment with his mate.

Chapter Four

On the outskirts of Haines, Alaska, Erik turned down a long driveway. They passed a large log building Maggie assumed was the pack house. There was a meeting happening tonight, judging by the cars gathered three deep in the parking lot. Another minute down the same road Erik pulled up in front of a tidy bungalow. An older home was tucked into the trees next to it. He opened her door and helped her out, his fingers caressing hers lightly as he held her hand a little too long.

Why did he have to make her tingle?

Maggie shook her hand free and turned to admire her sister's home. This was far quieter and more up her alley than living in a common apartment like some packs did. Being with a mess of wolves right now? Ix-nay. Not something she could handle.

Being cooped up with Erik for the past four hours made her more than ready for a little space from him as well. He'd done nothing but chat quietly to her about the Granite Lake pack, and ask polite questions. After the sensuality of the lunch they'd shared, all that danced through her brain were visions of them naked.

It had been a very long four hours.

A tall, lean figure strode down the stairs to greet them. Spiky black hair and a wicked smile flashed for a second before he snatched her up and spun her in a circle.

"Welcome. It's about time you made it north to join us." Tad released her, ruffling her hair. She returned his grin and simply stood next to him, relaxing into the calm his presence cast over her. It was amazing how his skills as an Omega soothed her jangled nerves. His brow shot upward and he hooted with laughter as he hugged them both.

"Erik! You old dog. Congratulations, both of you."

Oh shit. Another side effect of being an Omega—she'd forgotten he'd sense right away the potential connection between her and Erik.

"Tad—"

"Missy is going to be so excited to know you're mates. This is fabulous news."

"Tad—"

"Erik, you coming in as well? Or will you come back to get her later?"

"Tad, wait." Finally he stopped to listen, his head cocked to the side. The sensation of a cool breeze floated from him and she took a deep breath. The edge of her pain numbed as she took his hand. Omega skills ran deep in both her sister and Tad, and she'd never been more grateful for a calming touch. She had to speak quickly before she lost her nerve. "Erik's not staying with me. Not yet."

Tad raised a brow, concern written on his face. "Really?" He glanced between them for a few seconds before he shrugged. "Okay. Your choice. I guess we'll see you later."

Maggie turned to face the giant standing mere inches away. She kept her hands by her sides to stop from reaching for him and begging him to stay. "I..."

He tapped her lightly on the nose, his strong body and

gorgeous features so tempting and reassuring at the same time. Love and concern poured from him. "I heard you. Right now, I'll give you space. Say hi to Missy for me and I'll see you at dinner. You will sit with me."

She crossed her arms over her chest. *Bossy, arrogant...*

"Please." Erik winked at her, nodded at Tad and then strode across the deck toward the larger house on the adjacent property.

Maggie suddenly felt timid standing alone next to an Omega wolf—she wasn't scared of him, but he might be able to tell exactly what was wrong with her, and why. The reason for her attempt to return to the pack, as well as the reason she'd left in the first place. Was she ready for anyone to know it all?

For many years she'd been on her own, dealing with her fears. She still wasn't ready to admit to anything more than she needed help healing her body. Maybe in a few weeks, or months, she could talk about the rest of the trouble. Now it was enough she was attempting to rejoin a pack on a trial basis. She pasted on a bright smile before lifting her gaze to his. The expression on his face made her drop the façade. *Damn.*

"You know what's wrong with me, don't you? And why?"

He dragged a hand through his hair, staring off into the distance. When he looked back at her the anger and indignation she'd seen was once again controlled. He nodded slowly. "It's an Omega thing. Don't worry, I won't tell anyone, and I doubt Missy will pick it up. She's a little distracted right now. But, Maggie, you need to understand—you're safe here. Erik is a rock. You can share anything with him."

Tad's simple statement, and the lack of pity in his eyes did more to ease her fears than anything else. "Thanks."

"Now, we'd better get inside. Missy's a trifle...touchy these days. I'm going out of my way not to piss her off."

The house was clean and tidy except for a few toys scattered around. Bright pictures and fabric filled the cozy rooms. Maggie admired what she saw as they moved at a quick pace through to the back of the house. There the kitchen faced the trees, and just to the side was a cheery sunroom with floor-to-ceiling windows. Missy sat curled up in one of the comfy chairs, basking in the sunlight.

"Maggie? You're here!" Missy twisted in her chair and what Maggie thought was a pillow twisted with her. She threw her arms open wide, her eyes bright and her smile from ear to ear. "I can't believe you're finally here. Come and give me a hug."

Maggie raced across the room, maneuvering as close as possible, wrapping her arms around her sister and relaxing into her embrace. The tears that had threatened earlier fell now as they held each other for the first time in what felt like forever. Finally Missy patted her on the head and kissed her forehead.

"I'm so glad to see you again."

The heavy bulge of Missy's baby-filled belly separating them moved and Maggie pulled away in amazement.

"Oh my goodness, you're..." *Oops.* Gigantic was probably not a good thing to say to a pregnant woman.

"Huge? Damn it, I don't feel like a wolf, I feel like a stinking whale."

Maggie laughed. "There's never been more of you to love than now."

"Oh gee, good one. Like I've never heard that before."

They grinned at each other. The years apart faded away. Missy was family—all the family she had left—and she desperately needed family right now.

She reached out to give Missy's hand one more squeeze. "Thanks for letting me join you."

"You're going to be working for your keep, trust me. I can't move fast enough to keep up with Jamie. I'm so glad he won't be able to shift into a wolf until he's a teenager. He's hard enough to catch at eighteen months."

Maggie glanced around the room, looking for her nephew. "Where is he?"

"Sleeping. I think. I don't hear rockets going off, so he must still be locked in his room."

Tad dropped a kiss on his mate's forehead before squatting beside her. Missy glared at him. "Finally. Did you get me—?"

He thrust out a handful of brightly coloured chocolate bars. "Dark chocolate. Plus orange chocolate...with walnuts."

Missy stared, disgruntled, her mouth twisting. She planted both hands on the sides of her chair to heave herself into a new position. Tad rushed to help her. She smiled sweetly at him and started again. "After you left, I decided I also wanted—"

"—dried smoked salmon. There's one bag on the table. I left the rest in the fridge."

Maggie laughed behind her hand. "Missy, are you trying to be difficult?"

Her sister pouted. "It's his damn fault I'm a bloated beach ball. Again."

Tad winked. "All my fault. I confess." Maggie watched in amusement as the two of them teased and verbally sparred for a minute before he rose, kissing Missy's cheek once again. "I'm going to leave you two ladies alone to get reacquainted. I'll take Jamie with me, but we'll be back in time to escort you to dinner."

"I want pickles at dinner."

Maggie burst out laughing as Tad shook his head slowly. "You hate pickles."

"I want them."

Tad snickered at Maggie. "Pickles. At least it's not pickles and ice cream. That would be too cliché."

"Your fault," Missy restated.

He blew her a kiss. "I seem to remember you were there too." He ducked the pillow she threw and left.

The sun shining in made the room a warm haven of peace. To the side of the open window, an indoor water feature splashed and tinkled, the sound calming and reassuring. Missy adjusted herself, stretching her legs in front of her. Maggie stared in amazement at the perfectly round protrusion extending from her sister's stomach.

"You really are a beach ball."

"Shut up. Wait until you meet your mate and get pregnant. You're not much taller than me. There's nowhere for the baby to go but out, and this time with two of them..." Missy paused, then narrowed her eyes. Maggie felt her face heat up. "Crap, you've met your mate. Haven't you?"

Maggie leaned back in her chair and crossed her arms. "Anyone ever tell you it's damn hard to have a conversation with you when you seem to know everything, about everybody, before they tell you? It was bad enough when we were young, but since you've accepted you're an Omega, it's gotten ridiculous."

Missy snorted. "It's worse than you think. With Tad being an Omega too, we occasionally have really freaky conversations. Quit stalling. Who is it?"

Maggie stared out the window. "I'm not ready for a mate."

"Who is it?" Missy rubbed her hands together with glee. "Someone in Vancouver? Why didn't he come with you? Or is he making arrangements to move north too?"

Maggie stood and wandered away a few steps. She didn't need this. Not now. Did Missy not realize how difficult it was to be surrounded by wolves again for the first time in years? Had she forgotten what it was like to be truly afraid? The only reason Maggie had maintained any contact with their old pack was to keep in touch with Missy. As soon as Missy had mated with Tad, Maggie instantly severed all final ties with Whistler.

Her sister wouldn't drop the topic. "You met him in Whitehorse? Mags, you do realize this might be the solution to your problem."

Yeah, right. "Didn't you listen to me? I don't want to be tied to a mate. I'm still wondering if I made the right decision to come and be with your pack." She looked down at her sister. "How can you be so comfortable around all these wolves? After everything they did to you? All those years of your life wasted because our Alpha—"

"Oh, honey, I've told you this so many times over the past two years. *These* wolves have been nothing but kind to me. Our Alpha wasn't an Alpha—not in the truest sense of the word. Tad is more than twice the man my first husband ever was. I'm happy now, Mags, really I am. Yeah, it was a rotten situation, and I didn't deserve to be treated like that, but I've moved on. Isn't it time you did the same?"

The only person in the world Maggie knew who had gone through more hell than she had sat before her, huge with her second and third children. Living with a man she trusted, who went out of his way to make her smile.

Was it really possible to leave the past behind?

"Maggie. Tell me. Please."

It was impossible to resist her.

"Erik." Maggie squeezed her eyes tight as her body reacted to even saying his name. Her wolf woke again, this time with a slow and sensuous stretch itching up her spine. She hadn't felt that sensation in years.

Complete and utter silence greeted her announcement. She poked open an eye to see Missy sitting with her mouth gaping open. "What?"

Missy giggled naughtily. "You don't want to know."

"Bullshit. You made me tell you who it is, now spill. Do you not trust him?"

Her sister gasped. "Not trust Erik? The Friendly Giant? Girl, there is no one I trust more, except Tad and my Alpha. I was just imagining...umm...the two of you together. That's all."

Oh God. Not what she needed right now. "Great. I tell you I found my mate and the first thing that jumps to your mind is how we're going to manage sex. You're such a bitch."

They both laughed. "Yeah, well, sex is kinda up there on my 'things to think about' list these days since I'm not getting much."

Maggie rolled her eyes. "Enough. I haven't accepted the mating yet. I need to figure other things out first."

Missy lifted her belly with her hands and wiggled to the front of her chair. "What you're not taking into consideration is with Erik as your mate, he'll help you figure those *things* out. You need help, and he's the one able to give it. You need to trust him."

"Stop being a bloody oracle."

"I'm not being an oracle, I'm being an Omega. More importantly, I'm being your sister and I only want the best for you. Why are you fighting it so hard? Erik is a good man, and he's gorgeous. If I wasn't mated I'd be interested in a roll in the hay with him."

A low growl burst from Maggie. She froze in shock.

"Oops, looks like your wolf isn't as asleep as you thought."

Maggie dropped back into the chair opposite her sister. "No, she's getting more and more vocal, especially when it comes to Erik."

"That's a good thing."

The delight in her sister's eyes bothered her. *Get a mate, solve all your problems.* Maybe it just wasn't that easy. Maggie jerked to a standing position.

"So you say, but I'm not convinced. I only met him a few days ago. I need more time." She scrubbed her hands over her face, rubbing her temples. Her body and mind ached. Plus she wanted Erik so badly she could scream, but she was attempting to ignore those sensations. "I'm tired. I'm hoping to catch up on my sleep tonight before I hop into nanny mode for you."

Missy wrinkled her nose. "Heading to bed? Already? But we have plans for tonight."

Oh hell, no. "I can't do any big events yet. I only have to see you and Tad, right? At least for a while?"

Missy hemmed and hawed a few times. Something was up. "Dinner has been planned. The Alphas will be there. You can't insult Keil and Robyn and not come."

Shit. Her first night here and already she felt like running into the woods and hiding. She gritted her teeth together and spoke through tight lips. "Fine."

"There's the Alpha's brother, TJ. And...well..."

"Erik's going to be there, isn't he?"

"He goes where the Alpha goes, especially at formal events."

The only sound was the water tinkling in the fountain. Maggie turned to stare in horror at her older sister. "Formal events? What are you talking about?"

Missy sighed. "I'm really sorry, Mags, I didn't do it on

purpose. There's kind of this thing tonight. It's a big deal around the wolf community. I didn't realize the timing overlapped when you called to say you were arriving. It only happens every five years. I don't know if you remember from when we lived in Whitehorse before moving to Whistler. The AWG?"

"The Arctic Wolf Games? Those are now?"

"Yeah. The selection banquet for the Granite Lack pack is tonight. That's why there's a crowd of cars at the pack house." Panic must have shown on her face because Missy rushed to reassure her. "Honey, it's going to be okay. I'll sit with you, and Tad will, and we can leave as soon as they finish the announcements."

A shiver of fear rolled over Maggie. There was going to be a gathering of wolves and she had to go.

Welcome to hell.

She kept her back against the wall for as long as possible. Hidden in the shadows, she watched the pack members stroll around the large hall, chatting and laughing.

It looked safe. For now.

"You okay?"

She bit back a little scream. "How did you sneak up on me like that?"

Erik stroked a finger down her arm, his eyes sparkling with mischief. "I've been here for five minutes watching you. I thought you might like an escort back to the table. We're going to do the selection soon, and it will get a little noisy in here."

She swallowed hard. Somehow her fingers snuck their way into his. The warmth of his hand reassured her, calmed her slightly. There were a hell of a lot more wolves in the building than she had ever wanted to see in her life again. Still, she couldn't hide in the corner all night, no matter how much she wanted to.

"Okay." She stood straighter and held her head high. She might be shaking inside but there was no way she would let any of the pack know. Erik squeezed her fingers as he led her past the Alpha and his mate. The two of them smiled at her before turning their attention back to the man seated beside them.

"They like you." Erik pulled out her chair, next to Missy. He sat on her other side and draped his arm along the backrest. The curls of hair on his arm tickled the back of her neck and her nipples tightened. Great. She was freaking out with fear *and* getting aroused. His mouth was next to her ear. "I like you too. Very much." He licked her earlobe gently.

A shockwave raced through her system. *Shit.* "Stop that."

His soft voice tickled her ear. "I can smell your desire."

She elbowed him and he moved away slightly, chuckling.

Missy leaned over. "You okay? We can go now if you want. Seriously, we've put in our appearance, we can leave."

Maggie shook her head violently. She just wanted to get to the end of the bloody evening so she could curl up in a ball and collapse. But she refused to appear weak.

At the head table an older man in a business suit rose, a badge on his suit jacket marked with the initials AWG. He cleared his throat and the room hushed.

"The Arctic Wolf Games will begin three days from now in Skagway, Alaska. The rest of the teams have already been selected and are en route to the first challenge. The captain of the four-wolf team from Granite Lake will be selected first from a pool of ten hopefuls submitted by your Alpha. The other three will be filled by random selection. As always, the events involve both physical and mental abilities, so strength and speed are not the only abilities honoured.

"Every pack member over twenty is eligible. Your Alpha has already removed the names of those members who for one reason or another aren't capable of taking part in the Games. Like your Omega, obviously."

"Yeah, cause she'd kick their butts," some wiseass in the back shouted out and the room rang with laughter.

Maggie wrapped her arms around herself to keep her limbs from shaking. It was too noisy, too many bodies and just too much. She glanced to her right, her fingers itching to re-grasp Erik's hand. He returned her gaze, reaching to clasp her fingers and anchor her spinning world.

The chairman dug into the bag and pulled out a paper, holding it aloft. With great pomp he opened it and leaned into the microphone. "The first competitor, and team captain for Granite Lake, is—Erik Costanov."

Roars of delight filled the hall. Erik squeezed her fingers for a second before releasing them to stand and wave at the pack members who all cheered and clapped.

"Damn straight. Finally we'll have a chance at winning this thing."

Maggie looked at her sister in confusion.

"Granite Lake has never won. They've never even placed. The random-lottery method of selecting the team means most years there's been a team or two with a ringer. It looks like this time it's our turn. This is fantastic for the pack."

Something went cold in Maggie's soul. She might not be ready to take Erik as her mate but selfishly she wanted him nearby. "Will he be gone for long?"

Missy shook her head. "The Games themselves take about

ten days. You can always go along as a spectator." She smiled and touched Maggie's arm softly. "Are you thinking you'll miss him? That's a good sign."

Maggie shuddered. "I'm not going to hang out with more than a hundred wolves for a week. Tonight is bad enough, and it's only bearable because you're here."

"And Erik. Be honest."

Damn it anyway. Sisters were a pain in the butt. "Fine. It's easier when he's next to me."

Conversations filled the hall for a while as Erik chatted with the selection chairman. He smiled across the room at her like she was the only thing he cared about. Maybe...this would work out. Eventually. She knew better now than to deny her wolf, and the urge to get together with Erik grew stronger by the minute.

If only she didn't feel like vomiting from simply looking out over the sea of bodies in the hall.

The chairman repeated his routine, selecting another name from a larger bag this time. With a loud yell, a man somewhere in his late twenties threw himself into the air, clasping his hands over his head and shaking them in victory. He strolled forward, taking the time to stop and plant a kiss on a pretty girl near the front of the hall.

Missy leaned in again and whispered with a laugh. "Oh goodie, that's Jared. If there's a challenge involving getting into the girls' pants, we're now guaranteed a win."

Rather than watching what happened with the selection, Maggie was more intent on keeping an eye on Erik. He shook his new team member's hand then stood back, his gaze once again meeting hers. Calming her from across the room.

He was there for her. Could she believe that? She'd been taught all her life her wolf was an important part of her, not

51

something she could deny. She'd challenged that teaching to her own detriment. Maybe Missy's lovingly delivered lectures over the past two years had been right. Maybe it was time to move on.

Lost in thought she barely heard the chairman call the next name.

"Margaret Raynor."

Terror raised its head and choked her throat closed. "I can't..." Her voice was a ghost of a whisper. Confused questions rang throughout the room.

"Margaret who?"

"Is she really eligible?"

The Alpha stood and raised a hand. The chaos stilled as Keil looked out over the room. "She is eligible. Maggie officially joined the pack two years ago when her sister became Omega for Granite Lake. I have no troubles with her appointment to represent our pack." Keil's gaze stayed steady on her. His smile did little to calm the butterflies doing backflips in her belly. She didn't like attention from an Alpha, no matter what her sister said about the man.

The pack quieted at Keil's words, and everyone resumed eating and chatting. She couldn't do this. She'd ruin everything for the whole lot of them, and the Games were a big deal. More than a few curious glances were thrown her way as she excused herself and made her way over to Erik.

"I need to talk to you."

The pleasure in his eyes at her request hurt. She didn't want to be the one to ruin what should be a special day. She tugged him back into the corner of the hall. He knelt by her side so their heads were closer to level.

Oh shit, was she really going to tell him? She had to. She

grabbed him by the collar and put her lips inches from his ear to make her confession.

"I can't shift."

He'd wrapped his arms around her without her even noticing. Now his hands tightened where they held her waist. "What?"

She fought to get it out before she lost her courage and simply ran from the confining and overwhelming setting of the hall. "Some of the challenges are done in wolf form, right? I can't shift. I haven't for over seven years."

Erik stared for a moment before folding her closer, their bodies touching.

"Thank you for telling me." He kissed her forehead gently. "Don't worry about it."

Maggie gaped at him. "But...did you hear me? I can't shift. We'll automatically lose any challenge requiring us all to be wolves. I don't need a group of wolves pissed off at me. I need to decline, or whatever."

He shook his head. "You can't decline. If you step down, we compete with three. No substitutes are allowed. As for the rest, you need to trust me. Remember the mate thing? We're a couple and there's no challenge we can't face together."

His totally honest and straightforward answer did something to the block of ice enclosing her heart. Maggie reached out and latched onto his collar again, dragging their lips together.

Instant need. Passion and desire rocked her body. Moreover, she felt safe. Loved. His fingers tangled in her hair as he angled her mouth to the side, his tongue stroking her lips, her teeth, the roof of her mouth. They wrapped around each other in the corner of the hall, and she was oblivious to anything but the raging fire sweeping over her.

A roar rose from the crowd. A mixture of laughter, jeers and moans.

Maggie jerked to attention and squirmed back. The sound, so overwhelming and loud, frightened her and she clung to his forearms even as Erik released her. He cupped her cheek for a moment. He led her back to the head table, keeping her safely tucked under his arm. "What's the fuss?"

The chairman sniffed. "Didn't you hear the selection for the final member of your team?"

Erik glanced down at Maggie and grinned. "Nope. I was kind of distracted."

A long-limbed young man sauntered forward. Maggie frowned. He looked barely old enough to take part in the Games, although the resemblance to the pack Alpha was uncanny. So this was the younger brother she'd been told about.

"TJ?"

The gangly male flashed them double thumbs-up. "Hey, big guy. Let's win this thing!" He reached to give Erik a high five, and tripped over his own feet.

Chapter Five

The wind picked up as they left the natural harbor of Haines behind, cruising on the forty-five minute ferry ride to Skagway. Erik leaned on the railing and watched Maggie out of the corner of his eye. She sat by herself, away from where the rest of the group traveling to the Games lounged, laughing and goofing off.

He'd been busy the past two days. Not so busy he couldn't have made time for her. Hell, all he wanted to do was spend time with her, but she'd asked for space to prepare herself for the contest. He'd given it to her.

Now he wondered if it had been the right choice. The sweet kisses she'd bestowed on him had revved his motor and made him long for her to join him full-time—in his bed and in his life. Now she stayed back. Separating herself from him and holding to her fear like a coat of armor.

Funny how quickly his perspective changed. Until last week the most important thing in his life had been his position as Beta to the pack, and his friendships with Keil and Tad. His job? It had always been an extension of being there for people. He'd long ago dealt with his demons and life had been floating along just fine.

Until Maggie.

For a small package she was a bundle of trouble. She ran

hot and then cold, and both sides drove him nuts. Not only did the mate connection draw him to her, but he was used to protecting the weak. When she looked around, like she did now, with fear filling her pretty blue eyes, he could barely hold himself back from grabbing her and attempting to erase all her sadness.

Then she'd flip and get all tough and powerful, and that side was mighty attractive too. Both of them were strong wolves, and the temptation to see how strong she could be teased him. Sex between them was going to rock, if they could get past her freezing up every time he walked near.

The pack members wandered down the deck, leaving a clear path between Maggie and him. Pleasure filled him as she rose and made her way across the space, seeking him out. He opened his jacket to offer her protection from the wind. She wavered, her eyes dilating as she licked her lips. His body hardened.

She stepped back a pace and shook her head. "Don't do that. Not now. I'm barely managing to hold it together."

He shrugged. "Just thought I could warm you a bit."

She stuck her hands in her pockets and stared up at the sky. "We need to talk about this whole situation. How are we supposed to deal with the contests? I can't shift and I don't really want to be around all these wolves."

"It won't be as bad when we start the competition. Usually they have staggered starts for events, depending on what they are. You'll have only myself, Jared and TJ around."

She lowered her head and he caught his breath. The blue orbs were filled with tears. "I don't want to do this. Not any of it. I wish I could just go home."

Screw being patient. Erik stepped forward and gathered her in his arms. He held her, rubbing her back and trying to get the tight knots in her shoulders to relax. Whatever burden she carried was driving him crazy.

"I know you don't want me to say this, but sweetheart, you are home."

Maggie pushed herself away until she could look into his eyes. "I'm scared."

"I see that. But you're also very strong. You're also not alone. I'll do what I can to help you. Unfortunately, whatever it is you fear, we'll have to deal with eventually. The issue of your wolf, I'll worry about. Trust me."

"Trust you? Right." She paced away, her arms folded over her chest. She glared at him. "This mate thing really sucks, you know? Because as much as I want to just go hide, I can't help but want to be with you and it's part of what scares me."

Erik frowned. "Why would being with me scare you?"

Maggie hesitated.

Ah shit. "Is it because I'm so big?"

She dropped her gaze.

Great. Another instance of being judged at first glance. He hadn't expected it from his mate and it hurt more than he thought it would. He turned away to face the water. The demons were buried deep, but obviously not as completely gone as he'd imagined. Her opinion mattered a great deal.

A soft touch on his sleeve caught his attention. He looked down into her gentle face. "It's not your size. To tell the truth, I'm kinda...attracted to how big you are." She blushed and he coughed lightly. *Oh yeah.* She rushed on. "What I'm scared about is you going all wolfie on me and being overprotective. I don't need it. I can take care of myself."

He shrugged. "I won't go all he-man on you."

"Oh yeah? You can control the wolf so well you won't hurt

anyone who touches me?" She walked away from him, leaning her back on the sidewall of the passenger compartment.

This conversation grew more confusing by the second. "What are you talking about?"

"I saw it. In the Whistler pack, there was an incident. Tell me it wouldn't infuriate you if I...hugged someone. Or kissed them."

Holy shit. Missy had told them a few stories about her time in her old pack, but there were obviously more issues than he'd been aware of. He crossed to her side and knelt to take her hands in his, warming them between his palms. "I wouldn't like it, but I can behave responsibly. I don't think my reaction would be any wilder than a typical human man. I do have control. I've worked hard at it."

"Really?"

He nodded. "Really. Being the biggest guy around means there's always someone who wants to prove how tough they are by taking me on. I don't agree with violence as a first resort."

She stared at him for a long time, a curious expression in her eyes. A crowd of noisy tourists poured onto the deck and her gaze narrowed, her face growing red. What the hell was going on in her devious mind?

Maggie walked slowly toward the crowd, glancing over her shoulder as if making sure he watched. She tapped one of the young men in the group on the shoulder and smiled sweetly at him before saying something. The man shrugged.

She looked over her shoulder again, then grabbed the stranger. The whole group started talking loudly as she planted a huge kiss on his lips before releasing him and strolling back to where Erik stood.

He checked his blood pressure. He checked his temper. Both seemed normal, and the taunting look in her eyes did nothing but fill him with amusement. Okay, that was interesting. His wolf even snickered a little, seeing the humor in what she'd attempted to do. Contentment rolled over him. He really did have this under control.

Now he just had to deal with her underestimating him.

He lifted her chin with his finger so their eyes could meet. "Just what do you think that proved?" She chewed on her lower lip, a crease marring the space between her eyes. He hadn't reacted as she'd expected. "Should I go hit him? Fine."

"Erik, wait. I'm..." She grasped his hand. He patted her fingers gently before letting her hand fall away. He wandered over to the confused gathering, his amusement growing by the second. The men were speaking in Russian, and he understood their words with ease.

"What was that all about, Dmitri?"

"I don't know, but I think I like American girls."

Erik held out his hand and spoke to them in their own language. "Hello. My name is Erik Costanov. I'm sorry, my wife was teasing you. Are you enjoying your holiday in Alaska?"

He chatted with them for a while, the young men telling about the sights they'd seen on their cruise through the Inside Passage. He gave them a few recommendations for restaurants to try in Skagway and Anchorage. With enthusiastic pats on the back and lots of laughter, Erik said goodbye and returned to where Maggie sat on the stairs. She wiggled her nose and scooted over to make room for him beside her. They sat silently for a while. She turned her red face toward him.

"I didn't know you could speak Russian."

"There are a lot of things you don't know about me." Her scent rose and tickled his nose, and he took a deep breath, storing it for later. He could hardly wait to be able to sleep with her in his arms.

She spoke softly. "You just don't look like the type."

"Appearances can be deceiving. For example, you don't look like the type to get jealous easily, but I bet if I did what you just did, your wolf wouldn't like it very much."

She jerked upright and a faint growl escaped from her lips. Hmm, his suspicions were correct. Her wolf was there, just hiding. He'd have to think about how he could convince her to trust him so they could lure the creature back to the surface. After seven years, this could get rough.

Maggie nodded deliberately then a mischievous expression crossed her face. "Well maybe, maybe not. Tell you what, you go ahead and kiss that guy and we'll see what happens."

He laughed along with her. It was enough of a win for this time. Another of her defenses had fallen away, and when she leaned willingly into his side, his world grew a little warmer.

Maggie picked up the pack and fiddled with the straps, adjusting them again. There was nothing wrong with the backpack. The whole situation gave her the heebie jeebies.

"Are you nearly ready to go?"

She squealed and dropped the pack. How in the hell he managed to sneak up on her when he was so huge, Maggie could not understand. She nodded, grabbing at his hand to stop him from turning away. "I'm worried about passing out. What if I have a reaction while I'm on the hike and—"

"There are medical crews providing help if anyone gets hurt. You know that. This isn't a war game where we expect you to die in the field." He rubbed a circle on her palm with his thumb and a flash of heat ran up her spine. "You haven't had any troubles since the night of the banquet, have you?"

Maggie thought for a minute. He was right. Her last dizzy

spell had been back in Whitehorse. The last couple of days while she'd been at her sister's, getting ready for the Games, she'd felt fine. Felt the most energized and healthy she'd been for years.

"I feel..." The expression in his eyes sucked the truth from her lips. "I feel great."

He winked at her. "Wonder if it has something to do with being with other wolves. Like your sister suggested?"

Oh shit, no way. She looked around his bulk at the other teams standing in groups, waiting to begin the first event. The teams from Whitehorse and Denmark were already underway. The Tombstone pack stood at the line ready for their turn in the staggered start.

"I just don't want to make trouble for the team. I've brought my pills along in case, but I'm not going to be able to do this hike very quickly. I hope I don't disappoint you."

He crossed his arms for a moment, leaning his torso away from her. It was impossible to not admire the bulk of his arms, his biceps bulging his T-shirt. "It's not a race for speed. We have to solve puzzles as we go along. I expect you will be able to keep up just fine, and you're going to be a big help in contributing to us winning this event."

He spoke with such confidence her fears faded a little.

Erik motioned to the others. "Come on, team, let's take another look at the instructions. We have thirty minutes still until our start."

They gathered around, backs to the trees at the edge of the clearing. Before them the Dyea flats stretched to meet the ocean. The early-afternoon air was warm with the promise of heating up nicely. Erik spread out the map at their feet and traced the route they would follow. She was happy to see that once they started hiking, they'd be in the trees for the first third of the hike.

"Three days is the maximum time allotted to complete the thirty-three miles to Bennett Lake. That's a good solid hike, but it's not a race pace. We'll be going faster than the original Gold Rushers, but we don't have to carry as much gear. However, we not only have to reach the checkpoint in time, we have a series of clues to find. Some of them will be used later in the Games challenges."

"What if we can't find them all?" TJ asked.

"Missing one or two, we have a chance. Missing more will make the final challenge tough to win. So this isn't a sprint. We'll camp out for two nights and I really don't care if we see other teams passing us." He winked at Maggie. "It's not a race, although some of the other teams will try to convince you it is. This is a setup for later events. All we have to do is finish."

He pulled out the puzzle instructions, spreading them on the ground next to the map. Jared leaned a little too close and Maggie drew away, backing into the safety of Erik's side. He casually shifted his position, tucking her against his body and she relaxed. Why did he have to feel so good?

She looked down at the strange maps. Contour lines, altitude markers, not much else. "They're not giving GPS waypoints, are they?"

He shook his head. "We have to do this the old-fashioned way with only compasses and our noses. For this challenge, one of the team travels in wolf. They can shift back at night, but while on the trail and searching for clues, they have to be in their animal form."

Maggie's throat closed tight and she found it hard to breath. One of them was going to turn into a wolf. She had to be around a wolf.

She was going to die.

Without saying a word, Erik rubbed her back, a slow soothing motion. She closed her eyes and concentrated on the feel of his hand instead of thinking about the gnawing fear in her belly.

TJ cursed as his foot caught the edge of the paper and it ripped. "Damn it, sorry. Look, I'd like to volunteer to be the one who stays in wolf." He wrapped his long arms around his legs like he was trying to stop from touching anything near him. "I know I've got a bad reputation, but I am capable of pulling my own weight, especially if you keep me in my wolf form for most of the Games. It's just my human form that sucks rocks when it comes to coordination."

For the first time Maggie examined him more closely. He was as dark as his brother, the Alpha, but nowhere near as bulky. Long limbs, square jaw. TJ wasn't a bad-looking fellow, he just never seemed to be in the right place at the right time. There was a dark-coloured stain on his shirt where she'd seen someone bump into him and dump their ketchup-covered fries all over him.

Erik nodded. "I hoped you'd volunteer for the position, but not because I plan to keep you in wolf the whole time. You have an awesome sense of smell, and we need it for this challenge." TJ grinned, his limbs jerking in enthusiasm. Erik pulled the map out of range in the nick of time and laughed. "You're getting better. You've still got a little growing up to do, that's all."

The pleased expression in TJ's eyes made Maggie forget some of her own fears. Over the past couple of days every other time someone mentioned TJ's name, he had been called a klutz, whether he was standing there or not. Suddenly she felt indignant for him. What kind of crap was that?

"You just don't want to carry a pack." Jared poked TJ in

the side and the two of them fell to the ground to wrestle like puppies for a minute. A tug on her sleeve caught her attention and she followed Erik off to the side a few steps.

"I'm going to get TJ to change now. You okay?"

How did he know? "I...have to be, don't I?"

He stepped closer and spoke softly, for her ears only. "You think I haven't noticed you've tensed every time one of the other teams had a member shift? I didn't think it was because you were embarrassed by their nudity."

"Well, there was that one guy..."

"Hush." He kissed her nose, and she went all soft and melty inside. Three days on the trail with him. It was going to be heaven and hell. Oh no, they would be camping out. How was she supposed to avoid him in the evening? Avoid giving in to the attraction between them that grew by the minute? It was one thing to say she wanted to hold off on becoming mates, it was another to stick to her guns.

TJ stripped off his clothes and folded them neatly, slipping everything into one of the three packs waiting nearby. Maggie admired his muscular body. He might have two left feet in human form, but it was a pretty nice package of clumsy altogether. A low grumble from her left distracted her and she turned to see Erik staring, one brow raised. "You seen enough? Or do you want him to pirouette for you?"

No way. "Are you jealous?"

"Yes." The warmth he'd started earlier grew into raging heat. "I want you to be looking at me like that, not at TJ. I want to see admiration in your eyes for me—for your mate. It doesn't mean I'm going to go Rambo on his ass, but I'd appreciate if you'd stop drooling in front of me."

Maggie stepped into his body space and wrapped her arms around his torso, hugging him as close as she could.

"I'm sorry. I didn't mean to hurt you." Her instant need to comfort him puzzled her. Being in his arms satisfied something deep inside. Made her wolf rumble, low and needy. He stroked one hand down her back, the fingers of his other hand running though her hair. He held her for a minute, their heartbeats slowly synchronizing, and it felt so damn good she almost forgot where they were.

"It's okay. Apology accepted. He's a good-looking kid and an even better-looking wolf. You ready to meet him?"

She froze. TJ had shifted. Had Erik deliberately distracted her? Knotting her fingers in his shirt, she glanced over her shoulder. TJ sat on his haunches, his tongue lolling to the side as he panted in the heat of the noontime sun. His silver-grey fur shone, his eyes were bright and his nose twitched as he sniffed the air.

She reminded herself again—it was TJ. They were in public. Erik was nearby. "He is a goo...good...looking wolf...isn't he?"

She could do this. Only she wasn't doing it alone. She grabbed Erik, tugging him with her as she approached. She held out her hand, palm open like a person would with a strange dog.

"What the hell?" Jared muttered.

"Let her be," Erik ordered. He squatted to the side and ran his free hand over TJ's flank. She was squeezing the blood out of his other hand. TJ tilted his head to the side, confused, before sniffing her palm. His wet nose brushed her skin and goose bumps rose all over her body. He licked her fingers, then plopped on his belly at her feet.

And rolled over.

Her wolf howled with delight, fighting to take control, fighting to break free. A wave of dizziness rushed her. Erik's grip tightened and he moved to support her. "Okay?"

Wilderness. Starlit skies. Cool mountain water. The wind in her fur. Maggie ached for all the things she'd missed for so long. Again her wolf bumped the surface, making her blood sing, making the knot in her belly loosen a little more. She shook off Erik's supporting arms and reached for TJ, touching his chest, running her fingers along the stiffer fur of his muzzle. She took a deep breath and soaked in the scent of a wolf giving her obeisance. It felt good. Oh so very good.

"Granite Lake. You're up in ten minutes. You can take your place at the starting line." The Games Marshal passed them quietly, headed back to the officials' area.

TJ scrambled to his paws. Erik smiled at her as he helped her up. He kept hold of her hands. "Are we ready?"

He wasn't talking about the event. Maggie squared her shoulders and let the joy inside her shine out a little as she nodded. For the first time in years she felt like there really was hope.

Chapter Six

Maggie drew another deep breath of crisp mountain air into her lungs before quick-stepping to catch up. Erik walked ahead of them with TJ. She found herself surprised to be enjoying the chance to get to know Jared better.

"You've lived in the North long?"

Jared scrambled over a fallen log blocking the trail and turned back to give her a hand. The trail was in good shape, except for people with short legs.

"All my life. I've always been in the Granite Lake pack too. I can tell you, things have really changed in the past couple of years. Since Keil and Erik took over running things, conditions have improved so much."

He lowered her to the ground then motioned for her to walk ahead of him.

"What do you mean improved?"

"The old Alpha and his crew, they never took part in anything like the Games. Too far beneath them. It's not just special events like this one. Man, at times it's tough getting a job in Haines, but Erik and Keil have things arranged so there is never a chance for any of the pack to be unemployed." He laughed. "That doesn't mean you won't be working your ass off. They seem to be able to find the dirtiest, rottenest jobs around for the pack members who are slow to get their acts together.

No, it's been good to see the younger kids find a way to stay in the North instead of having to head south where their wolves aren't as happy. Plus the old timers? You see them regularly around the pack house now, where before they used to hide out since no one wanted to listen to them talk. Especially the real old geezers who forget they've told the same tale a million times."

She stopped to take a drink from her water bottle, thinking for a moment. It didn't sound like huge changes to her. Well, jobs were good, but she'd been thinking in the line of murder and other crimes being the issues, not laziness and neglect. "Did you know Erik spoke Russian?"

"Of course. He knows seven languages."

She jerked the bottle from her lips, the water sloshing down the front of her shirt. "Seven?"

Jared leaned back on a nearby tree, looking at her with a curious expression on his face.

"What?"

"You're very pretty."

She felt heat race over her skin. The admiration in his eyes embarrassed her and inside her wolf sniffed with disdain. "Thank you."

"Is there something between you and Erik? TJ swears you two are scented like mates, but..." He shrugged. "You're not acting like it. Just in case you're interested in a—"

"I don't want to get involved with you." Maggie's tongue tripped over itself in her hurry to turn him down. An icky sensation covered her at the thought of touching anyone but Erik.

Jared laughed out loud, his face split with an ear-to-ear grin. When he finally got himself under control he wiped the tears from his eyes and sucked in air. "I was going to ask if you were interested in a little advice. Sweetie, if you're scented to the Beta, I'm not going anywhere near you in a sexual way, even if you beg. I'd like to keep the family jewels intact and usable for a few more years."

She didn't think she could be any more embarrassed. All she'd done lately had been jump to conclusions. "Sorry." When she lifted her gaze, he was still grinning. "So, what's your advice?"

Jared shrugged. "You don't seem to know much about him. The mate thing is supposed to be cool, as in you're positive they're the only one for you. Yada yada. It works, I've seen it with the Alphas, and with others in the pack. I still think there's nothing wrong with a little good old-fashioned conversation to go along with the instant physical attraction and the lifelong chemical bond."

Maggie stood stunned for a moment.

"What? You look like I just suggested the two of you go bite heads off live chickens or something."

She snorted. "I'll confess your advice is not what I expected."

Jared adjusted the straps on his pack and pointed up the trail. He resumed talking as she walked beside him. "Why? Because you heard I like the ladies? I do, and if you weren't taken I'd be doing my damnedest to romance you. But I'm not stupid, I like more than a tumble. Sex is fun, but my hand is a lot safer than a regular routine of loving and leaving without more than a howdy-do and goodbye."

Maggie walked in silence for a minute before facing him. "That's good advice."

He winked. "But if you're not mates, then..."

She swung at him and he danced ahead of her, laughing.

She took a deep breath and followed. These wolves were different from what she remembered in her teen years. The posturing and constant one-upmanship weren't there. It must be because they were involved in the Games. This couldn't be how they lived all the time.

Could it?

TJ and Erik disappeared from the top of the next rise, heading off the trail into the bush. They must have found another clue. By the time she'd reached the heights, the guys were back, Erik sporting a rather large grin.

"You found another one?" Without thinking, Maggie leaned against him to check out the paper in his hand. His body was warm and solid, and she adjusted herself to nestle closer, tugging until the clue sheet was within her vision. He chuckled and she suddenly realized she was completely inside the circle of his arms. When she would have retreated, he subtly closed the space and trapped her, drawing her attention to the paper.

"Number eight. I tell you, the clues are logical but if TJ didn't have such a good sense of smell I think we would have missed half of them."

TJ lay flat out on the trail, panting lightly. His ears pricked up when Erik said his name, as if delighted by the praise.

Jared dropped his pack and passed out granola bars, unwrapping TJ's and tossing it to him whole. "Where was the clue this time?"

"On a tree."

"Drawn on?"

Erik shook his head. "Carved into the bark. Looks like it was done at least six months ago."

Jared swore. "How the hell did TJ get a scent on something that old? That's freaky impossible."

Maggie stared down at TJ and could have sworn he winked at her.

Erik laughed. "Yeah. The kid has always said his sniffer was good, and he wasn't kidding. We're at the point I think we should set up camp. I'd like to make an early start tomorrow so we have enough time at the end of the day to figure out the first mental challenge."

"You want to camp here?" Jared looked around. Maggie wondered too—there wasn't much of a clearing.

"Sheep Camp should be within the next half hour of hiking. Let's make that our destination. Once we get there, TJ can shift back and we'll get supper going." Erik turned her and Maggie froze. He reached and adjusted her chest harness straps then patted her cheek with his fingers before pointing for her to follow TJ's lead. She stared at him even as her body obeyed, and she took her first steps still watching his face. There was a laughing look in his eyes that made her want to haul him aside and ask just what the hell was going on.

She walked in silence for almost twenty minutes before it hit her. She'd spent the entire day with pack members, one in wolf, and she wasn't having a panic attack. She hadn't passed out and she was still safe.

Maybe Missy had been right. Maybe it was time to move on.

"So what do you think this is?"

Jared hit TJ over the head with his baseball cap. "Shut. Up. That's why it's called a puzzle, you idiot, because we don't know what it means."

"Jared." Erik didn't want to have to deal with a couple of young punks right now. Maggie reclined next to him and her scent filled the air. He'd far prefer to be able to continue the little mental fantasy he'd been enjoying than have to discipline his teammates.

"But he's asked the same damn question ten times already."

Erik sighed and sat up with reluctance. "I know. I'm only four feet away and I've heard him every single bloody time. As well as heard you make smart-ass responses and guesses back every single bloody time." He held out his hand. "Give me the puzzle page and find something else to occupy your minds. We don't have enough clues to be able to solve this, and you're both getting on my nerves."

The two young men exchanged panicked glances and then got busy. Jared grabbed a knife and whittled at a stick, while TJ produced a mouth organ from somewhere and started playing some pretty damn good blues. Erik always had appreciated that—even though TJ was clumsy, everywhere he went music followed.

Erik was just about to settle back down when there was a soft touch on his arm.

"You did that well."

Maggie sat with her arms wrapped around her legs, her face whiter than he remembered. *Shit.* "Did I scare you? I didn't mean to. The boys know I'm joking around."

She shook her head and frowned. "I'm not upset."

"You look pale." He shut his mouth quickly. What an incredibly stupid thing to say.

She rolled her eyes at him. "Gee, thanks. You're really batting a thousand right now aren't you?"

Yup. "Are you tired? Hungry?" *Can I massage your feet—or any other part of your body?* What he wouldn't give to be able to touch her. The whole day spent together, even hiking, had made his desire for her rise.

"No, I had more than enough at supper. I just need to think for a bit. Thanks for asking the comedy duo to shut up. I haven't been around a lot of people for a while and their constant yattering was getting to me." She stretched lazily and he enjoyed the way her T-shirt pulled tight over her breasts, the display making his mouth water. She might be a little thing, especially compared to him, but her breasts were full and distracting.

She curled up next to him, her hip touching his and he smiled. There was no way to ignore the physical pull between them. He wasn't even interested in trying to act as if it wasn't there. He'd go as slow as she needed, but he wouldn't back down. For the next thirty minutes he pretended to stare at the puzzle clues all the while looking over every inch of her body. She was going to be his—to care for and love and be with for the rest of their lives. The whole idea of fated mates didn't bother him one bit.

Jared yawned, a loud juicy sound that made Erik laugh. Time to round them up. "Hey, good job today, everyone."

TJ waved lazily, tucking away the mouth organ and letting out his own yawn. "It's the altitude, I swear it is. I'm heading to bed. Early morning I assume?"

"On the trail by seven please."

Jared nodded. "I'll turn in as well. I need to spend some time *talking* to my eyelids."

Erik wondered what the hell was up as Jared gave a direct look at Maggie as he spoke and she laughed.

It took a long time for the boys to crawl into the tent, and organize their sleeping bags with all their goofing off. The grumbles and laughter slowly died away, and Erik relaxed. Finally. Time alone with his mate.

The two of them sat silently, the small noises of the forest at night continuing. Here in the southernmost part of the Yukon, the sky insisted on staying bright, but it wasn't midnight sun by any means. There was a beautiful pink glow rising from behind the eastern mountain and Erik shuffled back down to rest his head on the log they'd rolled over to sit on.

Maggie looked at him for a long moment before sighing. "It's no use, is it?"

"What?"

She touched his arm hesitantly and a thrill shot through him. *Oh hell-o.* He kept his hands behind his head and watched as she wiggled closer, resting her head on his chest. Her short bouncy curls tickled his chin and her breath warmed him. "I can't deny I'm attracted to you. My wolf likes you too." She sat up to look into his eyes. "I just can't..."

"I'm not asking you to. Not yet. You told me to wait, I'm waiting." Shit, crap and merde, he was waiting.

"Where were you born?"

Erik wondered where the remote was. "That was a quick change of topic."

She snuggled against him and his wolf preened at the attention. "I just thought maybe if we learned a little more about each other, it would help."

He nodded slowly. Made sense. Didn't seem like they were going to be passing the time with any other distracting activities.

"Lavrentiya. Small coastal village on the Bering Strait."

She paused. "I guess that explains why you speak Russian. When did you come to Alaska?"

He told her about his childhood and moving around until the family finally settled in Sitka. "The rest of my family is still there. I'd love to take you to meet them. When this is all over."

"All over?"

"The Games."

"Oh." She nodded. "That would be...nice. I guess."

"What about you? I know your family went through some tough times, so let's not talk about that now. Tell me your favorite colour."

Maggie snorted. "You're really not what I expected, you know that?"

"Why? Because I want to be able to buy you sexy underwear in your favorite colour?" Her jaw dropped and he grinned. "Damn, you're fun to tease." She wiggled her nose and he wondered what was going on behind those beautiful eyes of hers.

He grabbed her hand. He'd done more handholding in the past few days than in his entire life before. "I was thinking about your fainting issue while we were on the trail. You said it's a chemical imbalance?"

She nodded. "It only got bad this past year, and obviously I can't shift to wolf for her to be able to heal me."

Yeah, that part. He wasn't even going to try to touch that issue yet. Soon, but not tonight. "I think it has to do with you not shifting and avoiding wolves. We give off so many pheromones, all the time, it helps maintain a delicate balance. Now that you're around pack, even a few of us, you should feel better."

Maggie stared at him. "That's why I came north to rejoin the pack. Missy insisted being around her family would be enough to heal me." She looked down at where their joint hands rested in his lap. "How did you figure it out? Do you have training in chemistry or something?"

"Nope. PhD in Slavic languages." She gasped in surprise,

her eyes widening and he laughed at her expression. "With a master's in Classic Literature."

"But...you work with Keil as a wilderness guide."

He shrugged. "When he looked into starting the company, he knew his brother would be too young to be a real help for a number of years. I offered to partner with him until TJ is able to take over."

"But why, if you have all this education..."

Maggie wrinkled her brow and he smoothed the skin on her forehead with his thumb. "He's my best friend. I'm currently tutoring a half-dozen students online, so I'm still using my skills, but it would have been very selfish to let his dream die when I could help him."

Her bright eyes examined his face closely, as if she was trying to see if this was some kind of trick to impress her. "You're a very complicated man, Erik Costanov."

He shook his head. "I'm as simple as they come. I believe in the golden rule, and I try to live by it."

She knocked him off balance by crawling across his legs and straddling him, her butt resting on his thighs. He lay very still, afraid to scare her, but savouring the sensation of her weight on top of him.

"What are you doing?" There, that managed to come out sounding reasonably intelligible. Damn, he spoke seven languages and right now English didn't seem to be one of them. His tongue was glued to the roof of his mouth.

She wiggled a little closer and he bit back a groan. Her hot core now rested against his groin and his cock rose like new bread in an oven. "I want to kiss you."

Hallelujahs rang in his brain. Holy freaking exclamations of jubilation, rejoicing and unending glee broke out in a full chorus. But when he spoke, he delivered a measured, "Okay."

She leaned forward and brushed her lips over his, and the electric sensation he'd felt before when they kissed buzzed through his torso and up his spine to his brain. Before he knew it, he'd buried the fingers of one hand in her hair, moving her the way he wanted her, while the other wrapped around her body to pull their torsos together. Her sweetness filled his senses, tantalizing his taste buds with the desire for more. Eager noises rose from her as their tongues brushed.

The night remained warm, and they both wore only shorts and T-shirts. Having a barrier between them was torture. He broke off their kiss, sat with her still straddling him, and whipped off his shirt. Her eyes bulged for a second before she reached down to caress his abdomen, the fleeting strokes tormenting him even as he savoured his mate finally, finally touching his skin again.

"Please take off your shirt." His voice cracked, he needed this so much. He closed his eyes against the disappointment of her saying no, then the rustle of fabric hit his ears. When he looked again, she still wore her bra, but the creamy smoothness of the rest of her skin more than made up for that small disappointment. He touched her reverently, stroking from her hips up the gentle indent of her waist until he covered the swells of her lace-covered breasts. She sucked in a gasp as he rubbed his thumbs in small circles over her nipples, the tips beading to tight points that stabbed his flesh through the fabric. "You're beautiful."

He ignored the driving urge to roll her over and take her, and instead slipped his hands back around her torso so their lips met again.

They kissed leisurely, exploring each other's mouths and necks, tongues stroking, teeth nibbling. Erik wasn't sure how long they sat there and frankly, he didn't give a damn. He'd waited his whole life for her, and they were finally doing what his wolf had been howling at him to do for days. Although the beast was going to be sorely disappointed when they didn't go all the way.

Maggie's breathing grew more rapid and she squirmed against him, her mound rubbing his groin like a firebrand. When he finally couldn't take it anymore, he grabbed her by the ass and adjusted her until he was happy. He ground them together again and again, and she moaned in his ear. Damn, he was going to come right like this if he didn't watch it.

So he lifted her and undid her belt.

She slapped at his hands. "What are you doing?"

"Take off your pants."

"Erik, we can't—"

He was on fire with a desperate need. "We're not having sex but I need to touch you. Take them off, now." She hesitated for just a second, then unzipped and dropped both her panties and her shorts, stepping out of the legs where they bunched around her ankles. She stood there, bare-naked except for her bra, with her pussy right in front of him and he had no power to resist.

He clutched her ass and buried his face between her legs. She cried out softly but he was too busy to warn her to stay quiet. Her sweet scent drew him, and he separated the curls covering her with his tongue and licked the length of her slit. Oh Lord, she tasted good. Her flavour raced through him and drugged his senses. He pressed his tongue into her pussy as far as it would go, lapping at the cream coating her passage.

She rocked against his mouth, opening her legs wider, her fingers clutching his head. The arm he'd wrapped around her ensured she stayed right where he could reach and delve into her body. She made the most delicious noises, and he stopped to take a deep breath and enjoy the sensation of holding her intimately.

"More," she demanded.

"Yes." He slipped a finger into her depths and suckled her clit with his mouth.

"Yessss..." Her hiss of agreement trailed off into the contented rumble of a wolf being petted and he smiled. He knew how to wake her wolf. When Maggie was ready, they would call her up together. For now, he wanted to bring his mate pleasure and concentrated all his attention on her. He teased the lips of her pussy with his fingers, circling the tender folds, before again plunging one, then two fingers in and out of her sheath. Running his tongue around the swollen bud of her clit, he flicked it repetitively with the hardened tip of his tongue.

A trembling started in her thighs, her knees shook and he lapped harder. He supported her with one hand as she cried out with her orgasm, a howling keen of delight that echoed into the still-bright sky. He dragged his fingers from her body with reluctance, the sticky moisture covering his hand calling like an aphrodisiac. He held her hips, giving her time to recover. The hands clasping his head softened their death grip as she caressed his short hair. He closed his eyes and planted a kiss on the tender skin in the crease of her thigh. Her scent filled every cell of his body and stopping now was the hardest thing he'd ever done.

A gentle tap on his cheek brought his attention to her bright eyes filled with passion and gratitude. "That was amazing."

"For us both."

She giggled. "I guess this proves I really am a wolf at heart. Damn, I can't even feel embarrassed everyone within a five-mile radius knows I just climaxed."

They laughed together as Erik pulled up her undies and helped her with her shorts. Their hands brushed and bumped and tangled as he took advantage of every touch he could sneak in.

She dropped back onto his lap, her arms draped around his neck. "Thank you."

"My pleasure." It had been. Her gaze dropped to his crotch and the obvious swell remaining behind the fabric. "Yes, I still want you."

Maggie nibbled on her lower lip. "Not yet. I'm sorry, that sounds so selfish of me, but I'm not ready."

"But soon?"

She hesitated. "Maybe."

His heart leapt. Maybe was way up from no. "I can live with maybe."

He kissed her one last time, just to drive himself insane, then led her to the tent. Morning would come soon enough.

Chapter Seven

"We've got a problem."

Maggie groaned as she sat up from where she'd sprawled on the side of the trail. The past two hours had been sheer hell as they slogged their way to the top of the Golden Stairs and over the Chilkoot Pass. She hadn't hiked so much vertical ascent since she was a teenager, and every muscle screamed in protest. "What's wrong, Jared?"

"Did TJ lose a page of the puzzle when he was goofing off last night?" Jared frowned as he flipped through pages. Erik reached out and Jared handed them over. Maggie watched in concern as Erik examined the set. Jared growled in frustration. "If King Klutz—"

"That's enough." Erik cut in sternly and Jared had the grace to look sheepish. "There's nothing missing. What's the issue?"

"There are no additional clues for the last few spaces," Jared pointed out. "There are also no landmark clues. Three completely blank columns—it's like we're going in blind and have to find a needle in a haystack." Maggie crawled closer to look over Erik's shoulder at the papers. She leaned against his strong back, the warmth of his body drawing her like a magnet. The whole day she'd forced herself to stay away from him but now gave in to the need to recharge her batteries with a brief touch. He glanced at her and winked, and she blushed. Their sexual attraction was normal for wolves, but her continued denial of their mating and his patient response confused her. She felt like a broken fan, running hot then cold.

"I noticed the first day. We'll figure it out tonight." Erik handed the papers back to Jared. The young man stared in shock.

"How can we fill in the missing answers without clues or landmarks? Why didn't you say something earlier?"

Erik shrugged. "There was no use in panicking. The challenge must be solvable, so I decided we'd figure it as we went along."

Jared shook his head. "You really are too cool and collected at times, aren't you?"

A muffled howl rose from up the trail and they turned to see TJ racing back. His loping gait tore up the rocky terrain as he returned to drop a rock at their feet. Erik picked it up, running a hand over TJ's head. "Well done. I wasn't looking forward to hunting for this answer."

"Where was it?"

He pointed to the mountain spine extending another mile off to their left, the razor edge jagged against the skyline. "The puzzle clue was *Cutting you off* and the map shows the location to be along the far ridge. I sent TJ ahead in the hopes the answer would be something obvious, and save the rest of us the trip."

Maggie swallowed hard. Imagining having to hike the ragged rocks to the spire made her even more grateful for TJ's wolf. "I would never have made that."

"What symbol do I add?" Jared asked.

Erik handed the rock over to Maggie and she turned it over

carefully. "There's nothing carved on it." Her stomach fell. Were they going to have to do the dangerous climb after all?

"Don't worry, this is what we need. It's not always simple like having the answer written on the surface. Remember the answer to the sixth clue involved a math formula." Erik nudged her arm. "What kind of rock is it?"

TJ pawed at her feet and she knelt to scratch behind his ears as she stared at the stone chip. "You wouldn't have brought it unless you thought it was the answer, so I'll assume it wasn't in a normal setting." She wrinkled her nose. "It sparkles, so I'll guess it's fool's gold. There's got to be a lot in these parts."

Erik laughed. "Remind me never to go panning with you. You'd miss out on a bonanza."

She gaped at him. "It's real gold?"

"Yup, and that's not the usual location to find a nugget. Gold is rarely found loose like this, and never up that high. Someone had to have planted it there."

Maggie rotated the chunk again. "Still doesn't look like much to me."

Jared added a few notes with a flourish. "One piece of gold." He glanced up, worry back on his face. "There's only three more clues before we run out and hit the blank section of the puzzle."

"Then we'll stop for the night." Erik rose and held out a hand to Maggie to assist her up. She took it gratefully. "That's the last of the big uphill. From here on it's rolling trail until we start down to Bennett Lake. The next clue is *Reflections* and the coordinates look like it should be by a water source, so let's get moving. The day will be done before we know it."

He held up her backpack and Maggie crawled under the shoulder straps reluctantly. He brushed his hands over her body as he helped tighten the snaps and buckles, and her skin tingled.

"Stop it," she whispered. Great, now she was going to be hiking with sore feet, tired muscles and an aching need in her belly.

Erik chuckled. "I'm just trying to be helpful."

She elbowed him.

"But it doesn't mean anything." TJ scratched his head.

"It has to." Jared paced back and forth and Maggie rubbed her temples. They'd set up camp two hours ago, had dinner and then the puzzle began to drive them all nuts.

"They are totally unrelated words. It's gibberish, no matter which way we read them."

Maggie stared at the papers at her feet. It was true. There was no logic in any of the words and symbols they'd found. "We've tried rearranging the words. We've taken the first letter, the last letter. We've..."

"...tried everything." Jared glanced over at Erik. "What if we don't figure this out? Can we finish without the last six clues?"

Erik nodded slowly. "We just need to get to the Bennett Lake check-in by three. That's not a problem at all. Only in previous Games, the final challenge used information gathered from all the rest of the events. Five years ago the team in fourth spot came from behind to win because none of the leaders had all the clues."

Maggie sighed. She'd felt so useless this whole challenge. Unlike TJ who had more than pulled his weight, all she'd done was ensure they hiked slower than usual. Usually she was good at logic puzzles. She picked up the clues and shuffled through them again. Something caught her eye.

"Erik, what are these notes?"

He sat next to her and she soaked in his presence. "Those? I kept track of where we found the answer. I figured everything might help in the end."

Her heart raced. "What if the clues weren't just to help us find the location, but we have to use them twice?"

Jared plopped down across from them, hope shining on his face. "How do you use a clue twice?"

Maggie laid out the paper and pointed. "We found the answer to number eleven by looking in the reflection of the pool at the base of the waterfall, right?"

"There was the Greek symbol omega. We wrote it down. It means nothing."

She nodded. "But when you look at your reflection it comes out backwards." She wanted to jump up and down. This was the right track, she was sure of it.

Erik brushed her arm. "But the symbol for omega is the same whether you draw it backward or forward."

Maggie laughed. "But what if you think of it as the back of the alphabet? Omega is the last letter of the Greek alphabet. What's at the other end?"

TJ shot up his arm before lowering it slowly. "Sorry, too many years of school training. Alpha is the Greek A."

"Right." Maggie started a new paper. She deliberately drew the symbol for alpha. "And here...we wrote down *gold*. But the clue said *Cutting you off*. The chemical formula for gold is Au. If we cut off the U we get an A."

The next thirty minutes passed in a blur as they struggled through the rest of the puzzle, discovering as they fed the current answer through the clue again there were clear-cut alternatives.

"In your notes you recorded what height we found the answers, high up or low to the ground. Should I add that information?" Maggie glanced at Erik to find him staring at her with a twinkle in his eyes. "What?"

"You're very attractive when you're obsessed about something."

Jared laughed. "You two. Save the lovey-dovey for later. Let's solve this thing."

When the new list was finished, Maggie held it up with a flourish. Now they would be able to find the final answers. She scanned the page quickly and her hopes fell. There was nothing but a series of single letters from A-G mixed up again and again.

It still made no sense.

Jared and TJ started laughing, and her temper flared.

"It's not funny." So much for her being an asset to the team like Erik had suggested.

"We tried. I guess we'll just have to finish without the final information." Jared threw a rock into the bush and lay back on the ground in disgust.

TJ startled. "What are you guys talking about? Don't you see it?"

His earnest expression made Maggie feel even worse. "There's nothing there that helps us, TJ."

He snorted and took the paper from her to scrawl down six more letters.

Erik looked at the list and raised a brow. "You think?"

"Positive." TJ nodded rapidly. He scrambled in his pockets, fumbling as he pulled out his harmonica. As the first notes of the familiar children's opera rang into the air on the unusual wind instrument, Maggie laughed.

"No way, you're saying those letters are musical notes? That tune is too funny."

Erik grinned at her. "I think TJ's hit on the right solution. Does it help if I tell you the race director's name is Peter?" He clapped slowly. "Well done, team."

Jared groaned. "*Peter and the Wolf*? We went through all that searching to have to listen to TJ playing bad classical music on his harmonica?"

TJ hit him and the two of them tumbled away to wrestle again. Erik smiled down at her and she grinned back in satisfaction. She really had managed to help the team.

Suddenly the idea of being a part of the pack didn't nauseate her. The guys had been nothing but supportive of her, and her heart no longer went into palpitations when she remembered she was in the bush with three other wolves.

Except for the rushing, pounding rapid beat of her heart that remained every time she thought about Erik. Her wolf bumped to the surface, as if reaching for him. His eyes widened as they stared at each other, and Maggie had to hold back from pressing closer, rubbing herself all over him. For one moment she seriously considered dragging him into the tent and accepting their mating.

Her throat closed tight and she dropped her gaze away, fidgeting with the papers. She organized them, then thrust them out at him.

The idea of being in wolf form with others around—she wasn't sure she'd ever be ready for that step. Mating with Erik but refusing to let their wolves have contact would be the cruelest thing imaginable. She couldn't play games with his emotions, couldn't tease his wolf with promises she was unable to keep.

What of the challenges still to come in the Wolf Games? Had she helped solve this puzzle only to tear victory from their grasp when she was unable to shift?

"You're thinking too hard. Let it rest." Erik brushed a stray hair back behind her ear and she leaned into the caress without thinking. "In fact we all should turn in. Just because we know what we're looking for won't make tomorrow any easier."

"So using the song to solve the puzzle gave us six letters in the answer column, but no idea where we'll find them? I assume that's the information we'll need for the final event, right? That sucks," Jared complained as he unzipped the fly to the tent.

"Hey, at least we know what to look for, and with TJ's great sense of smell, I'm confident we'll be at the checkpoint in plenty of time." Erik patted TJ on the back, catching him by the shirt when he tripped. "Yup, a good night's sleep and a short hike tomorrow. I'm betting there will be little time between the end of this challenge and the start of the next."

Erik settled the boys, returning to hold his hand out to her. "As much as I'd love a repeat of last night, I suggest we hit the sack as well."

She nodded slowly. There was too much to say and she didn't have the strength yet. "Erik, what if I can't—?"

He held up a hand. "I'm not trying to be rude, but I'd like you to trust me on this one. Sleep first, discussions later. You did so well with the puzzle, but I can feel your exhaustion from here. While you're getting the chemicals you need from being with us, I doubt you've hiked this far in the past few years while hanging out in Vancouver." He pulled her against his body and she molded herself to him. It felt so wonderful. He lifted her chin and stared at her. "I'm warning you I'm going to hold you tonight. I can't resist, and I think you need it too. If you were planning on protesting, argue here so we don't wake the boys."

Jared's snores already rocked the tent and Maggie laughed. "Like me blowing a trumpet in his ear would wake him." They exchanged grins before she grew serious again. There was nothing she wanted more right now than to feel his arms around her. "I could handle you holding me. If you feel you absolutely must."

He nodded seriously. "I think it's vital."

They slipped into the tent and Maggie relaxed, the warmth of her mate covering her like a blanket as the never-ending light shone through the walls of the tent, filling the space with a peaceful blue glow.

Chapter Eight

Erik was pleased when their team finished the challenge in plenty of time, finding all but one of the puzzle pieces. Maggie had insisted on recording everything she could think of about the locations where they'd discovered the letters, hoping the information would help them down the road. They barely crossed the line at the checkpoint before they were whisked away to Carmacks to start the next race.

He kept Maggie beside him as they boarded the bus with four other teams. The fear in her eyes made his heart ache, but the way she squared her shoulders and insisted on sitting with TJ filled him with pride.

The chairman rose at the front of the bus to announce the details of the next challenge.

"You'll all be in human form for this event of the Games."

A murmur carried through the bus and TJ swore under his breath. Erik dropped a reassuring hand on the young man's shoulder.

"You'll be paddling through one of the toughest sections of the Yukon River. Because of changing water levels, the Five Finger Rapids are nowhere near as dangerous as they were in the days of the Gold Rush. But we've planned a mass start, so there will be a lot of canoes vying for the safest route. It's up to you to make it through to the other side in one piece.

"Scoring for this event will involve both time and bonus points. There will also be deductions." He held up a brightly coloured float. "We've got six buoys anchored at various points along the river. If you get close enough, you'll once again have an opportunity to observe a symbol that will help you later. It's completely discretionary if you wish to attempt to reach the buoys."

"What would cause a deduction?" one of the Anchorage team asked.

The chairman grinned at them, his canines long and sharp. "Falling out of the canoe. You can still get a time score when your canoe crosses the finish line, but anyone out of the canoe causes a deduction to be applied, no matter how it happens."

TJ's shoulder tensed even more under Erik's hand. The kid was just going to have to get over his fear of screwing up. So he was clumsy—he was way better now than a few years ago.

The chairman sat and a low rumble of voices filled the bus. Erik leaned back in his seat trying to get comfortable for the journey, his knees cramped against the back of the bench in front of him. Even the buses adapted for wolves were too small for his bulk. He sighed and closed his eyes.

When he opened them again they'd arrived at Carmacks. He herded his crew over to the side of the staging area then stood back to take a good look at the setup. The canoes were lined up along the edge of the river, twenty feet from the shoreline. Erik eyed his opponents with a practiced eye, spotting the three teams who would be the most competition in this event.

TJ remained silent as Jared joked around. Without her saying a word, Erik knew exactly where Maggie stood, hiding behind his back, sneaking peeks around him at the other wolves. She was doing extraordinarily well, not panicking as the group grew larger by the minute. All the teams were assembled and their support crews were placing the final supplies in piles for the teams to collect when the whistle sounded.

Arms wrapped around his waist and he stilled, covering her small hands with his own. She'd buried her face in his back, her breath warm against his skin. Small tremors shook her body and he twisted, kneeling down to enclose her in his embrace. They stayed there for a moment, just breathing each other's air. It felt so damn right to hold her.

He kissed her forehead gently. "You going to be okay?"

She nodded quickly. "I might throw up a few times, but I'm not giving up." Her stubborn announcement made his heart sing. They were truly going to be a wonderful pair, once they dealt with a few minor issues like her shifting problem. Her refusal to accept their mating. Making sure—

Jared nudged them, breaking them apart, before handing over two life jackets. "Try to throw up over the edge of the gunwales."

Maggie smacked him on the arm and Erik bit back his surprise. "Next time, don't listen to a private conversation. If I have to throw up, I'll throw up anywhere I damn well please. Got it?"

A ripple of shock crossed Jared's face and he dipped his head in submission. Maggie stood just a little straighter and Erik hid his grin. It seemed his little wolf was starting to feel her place in the pack.

He turned to make sure TJ had his lifejacket on properly. The boy was still swearing colourfully, with few repetitions.

"Does your brother know you're this talented with words?"

TJ snorted. "Who do you think I learned them from? Well, him and Robyn. She's awful good at cussing in sign language."

"What's wrong?"

"I'm going to fuck this up. I just know it. I'm going to cause some major catastrophe."

"Why?"

TJ looked at him like he'd grown a third head. "Because I'm *me*. You know I can't walk twenty feet without landing on my face."

Erik shrugged. "You bounce pretty good. Just get up and get your ass into the boat." He tightened TJ's lifejacket straps and stepped back to complete his own.

TJ continued to stare. "How can you be so calm when chances are I'm about to screw this up for us like I always—"

"Enough." Erik let his power roll out over the young man as he towered over him. "I don't let anyone talk shit about you, not even you. Do your best, that's all any of us ask. If you do have an accident then fix it the best way you can."

The panic in TJ's eyes faded slightly.

A piercing whistle broke the air and the team gathered around Erik.

"Okay, there's the five-minute warning. Those are prospector canoes—flat bottomed so they're nice and stable. I want Jared in front, TJ and Maggie side by side in the middle. I'll take the stern and steer us. What do you think about going for the extra buoys? Yes or no?"

TJ flicked a glance at the team. "I'm just going to paddle and keep my ass in the seat. I'll do whatever you decide."

Maggie chewed on her lip. "Are the buoys far out of our path?"

Erik shook his head. "Looks like we can pretty much stick to the current. We'll want to do that anyway to make the best time. The fastest route down the river is not a straight line.

93

When we get close to the rocks we'll have to stay to the right." He looked at Maggie. "Did you ever see the rapids when you lived in Whitehorse?"

"If I did, it was a long time ago."

"There are four towers of granite dividing the current into five parts. The far right is the best one to go through, but the main thing is to avoid the towers themselves and the far-left channels. There are sweepers off the left, and some nasty undercurrents over there. When we get close, just listen to my instructions. We'll use the first few minutes in the canoe to practice our strokes."

"What about the symbols?" Jared jiggled on the spot as he stood waiting.

"Maggie, I want you to try to memorize them. Describe them out loud when you see them and we'll all try to help remember, but I don't want all four of us staring at the damn things or we'll be in the drink for sure."

The final warning whistle blew and there was no more time for discussion. The gun went off and they were away, racing over the grass to grab paddles. They sprinted to the side of the canoe to manhandle it down to the water's edge. Jared hopped in, TJ fell in and Maggie gracefully jumped over the side as he pushed them out into the current.

"I hate wet socks." Jared complained from the front of the canoe.

Maggie laughed at him. "You're not wearing socks."

Erik laughed. "Okay. Practice time. Everyone draw on the right."

They practiced maneuvering the canoe until Erik felt they should at least survive the trip. The rest of the competitors had settled into a pattern around them. There were two canoes alone in the lead, a group of six or seven close around the

Granite Lake team, and another larger pack behind them.

"Buoy approaching on the right," Jared shouted.

Erik checked the river. "We'll try for this one, then we need to slip over to the left more."

Three other canoes all veered the same direction and suddenly the river grew crowded. Erik steered their craft to the side but it was too late. One canoe rammed them in the bow, another slammed into the other side.

"Shit." TJ's paddle went flying. He managed to grab the seat, the boat rocking as he attempted to regain his balance.

Erik ruddered hard, even as Maggie's quiet voice rose over the confusion and shouts of the other teams. "I saw the symbol. We can go."

They pulled away from the mess of boats. Once they were back in the current, Erik reached under his feet and poked the swearing TJ in the back with a spare paddle.

"You eat with that mouth? Here." The look of delight on TJ's face made Erik grin. "Just hold on to it tight, okay? We've only got one spare left."

"I thought you were going to call out the symbols, Maggie?" Jared glanced over his shoulder at her.

"I figured just in case someone didn't see it, I shouldn't announce it for them all. It looked like a cowboy hat with a triangle underneath."

The crowd of boats slowly spread out. Clusters of twos and threes still paddled beside each other, but with each buoy Granite Lake managed to lose another of their closest competitors. They made it past three more buoys before Erik decided it was enough.

"The rapids are around this corner. I think we should just concentrate on finishing strong and not worry about the final clues."

The team was silent for a minute before Maggie spoke. "I *am* getting tired."

Jared nodded. "I vote for finishing. If you noticed the canoes ahead of us, not one of them stopped to get any of the extra clues. I think the four we saw is enough."

They settled into a paddling pattern. There was a certain joy in moving in synchronization with the group this way. Not as good as running in a pack, but with a rhythm and a beauty to it all the same. Erik admired Maggie's arms and shoulders as she paddled, watching the way her muscles moved under the skin. He'd love to see her body shifting like that on top of him, rocking from side to—*damn*. This was not the time to get distracted thinking about his mate.

He steered them toward the safest channel just as a loud ruckus behind them made him check over his shoulder. *Oh shit.*

"Holy crap! Did you see that?" Jared gasped his surprise.

"Eyes forward, Jared. You need to keep to your task as lookout."

"But they dumped the other team!"

Erik shook his head. "Keep paddling, crew. Yeah, we've got a group trying an unusual method to gain points. Concentrate on the river in front of us and let me worry about the cheaters." TJ and Maggie exchanged worried glances before paddling madly. "Whoa, no rush. Just paddle. Trust me."

He laughed. He'd wondered when someone would get creative. While wolves followed a strict code of conduct in governance, one of the sub-rules was if you were powerful enough, you could make your own rules.

Another shout rose from behind and he watched for a

moment as the cheating team came alongside their next victim and made short work of tipping them over. Erik considered a defense and decided they'd never know what hit them.

"TJ, you remember when we guided that family reunion down the Stikine?"

"Are you freaking kidding? I still have nightmares...no, oh no. Holy shit, you can't be serious—?"

"On my command."

"Crapola. Yes, sir."

"Erik. What's happening?" Maggie sounded frightened and he wanted to reassure her, but there was no time. In a rush the other canoe was at their side, three of their team all at the ready to grasp the side of the Granite Lake craft.

"Now?" TJ asked, his voice coming out high and squeaky.

"Wait for it." Erik glanced over at the captain in the rear. He should have known. "Darren. Having a good time so far? You and the team?" There weren't many people Erik actively disliked, but Darren topped his shit list.

The captain of the Anchorage team startled at Erik's bland response, then grinned widely, his canines showing. "Wonderful time. We'll see you at the finish line, dripping wet."

Erik shrugged. "If you insist. Now, TJ."

TJ leapt, his long limbs propelling him into the air and over the side. He came down hard in the neighbouring boat.

Maggie squealed as their canoe rocked. Jared dropped into the bottom to help stabilize it. Erik threw himself down as well, cracking his paddle on the knuckles of the other team where they clasped the gunwales. Shouts of pain rang out, the hands released and with a clatter the boats sprang apart.

"What the hell—?" Darren's angry shout was following by an enormous splash.

Erik, Maggie and Jared sat up slowly to watch the opposing team flounder around their capsized craft. Somehow their canoe had flipped over completely and TJ clung precariously to the bottom, his arms and knees spread like he was in his wolf form. Erik snickered in appreciation at Darren's expression until a change in the roar of water alerted him. They all spun to see the towers of rock rapidly approaching. They grabbed their paddles and slid back into position.

"Draw on the right, Maggie. Jared, forward on the left. Don't panic, we've got time."

"What about TJ?" Maggie asked, concern tingeing her voice.

"He's probably going to get wet. We figured it was a very real possibility from the start. Hard! Paddle hard!" Erik judged the distance to the approaching rocks. Finally they were in the correct line. *Good.* They still had time. "Back paddle. Now."

The rush of water forced them forward no matter how much they struggled against it, but there was enough difference in momentum that the canoe carrying TJ caught up to them. It could all be for nothing if this didn't work. Erik knelt on the bottom, his knees spread wide to try to reduce the coming rocking. "When I call out, brace yourselves."

Erik took a deep breath. He reached out his hand and grabbed TJ's wrist. "Now!" One solid yank brought TJ flying across the space between the canoes, his arms and legs flailing wildly. He landed in a heap in front of Erik, gasping for air as the other canoe flipped and filled with water.

"Erik!" Jared shouted a warning.

There was no time to do anything but pick up his paddle and slam it into the water. Erik leaned hard, using the blade like a rudder, steering them away from the rapidly approaching rock formation. Jared whooped as a sudden cross-eddy dragged them past the jagged rock edges to the safety of the downstream side.

They all sat back and let the current carry them, the canoe spiraling in a gradual 360-degree circle. Erik sucked in a calming breath and stared up at the sky. The adrenaline rush faded, his pounding heartbeat slowed.

A loud cheer rose from the people watching along the observation platforms as Granite Lake crossed the finish line. Erik brought them into the docking area set up farther down the river, more than satisfied with his team's efforts. Maggie and Jared scrambled out first, chatting excitedly as they waited on the dock for him to join them. He picked Maggie up and spun her in a circle, his heart jumping as she gave him a big juicy kiss then hung onto his neck, grinning with delight.

"That was awesome. Can we do it again?"

He laughed. "I knew you had an adventurous streak. You didn't even throw up."

She dropped her head on his shoulder and spoke quietly. "I'm not happy about being with the other wolves, but being with you feels better and better. I...like you, Erik. I like your sense of justice."

Her confession thrilled him more than finishing another challenge. He squeezed her tight before carefully putting her down, keeping one arm draped around her shoulders to block her from the other teams walking by. Glancing into the bottom of the canoe, he found TJ still lying there with his eyes closed, a huge grin pasted on his face.

Erik squatted by the side of the dock. "You planning on coming with us? Because I can send out for a pizza or something if you're staying the night."

TJ opened his eyes and let out a big contented breath. "I didn't screw up, did I?"

Erik laughed. "No. You did just fine."

TJ sat up and nodded. "Maybe there's hope for me after all."

"Maybe." Erik stood and reached for Maggie. She slapped a hand over her mouth and her eyes popped open wide just as a loud splash rang out.

The canoe drifted away down the river as TJ clung to the mooring rope. He bobbed up and down in the water, swearing softly. A huge sigh escaped him. "Then again, maybe not."

Darren and his team sloshed past, their faces grim. The leader turned to glare at Erik, his gaze raking Maggie's body. Erik stepped in front of her slightly. He didn't want the ass anywhere near her. Not when she'd come so far in facing her fears.

"Nice teamwork, Erik." Darren growled. "You going to introduce me to your lady?"

Maggie ducked under his arm, her face buried in Erik's side. "Looks like she's not interested. Keep walking, there's nothing here for you."

Darren raised a brow, his gaze flicking between Erik and the little bit of Maggie still showing. "Interesting. We'll see you in the next challenge."

They stomped off, their dripping bodies leaving a trail behind.

Chapter Nine

Maggie knocked on the door of the hotel room next to hers, her heart beating loud enough she was surprised they couldn't already hear her standing outside. She didn't really want to do this, but since she saw no alternative, she was going to put on her big-girl panties and force herself to have a good time. If she didn't pass out first from nerves. Jared opened the door and whistled in appreciation.

"My oh my, you clean up nice."

Maggie spun in a circle, the layers of her skirt floating around her. Now that she knew he was safe, Jared reminded her of nothing more dangerous than a golden retriever. "Why thank you, kind sir. Is the rest of my harem ready to escort me to the ball?"

He snorted and gestured her in. "TJ's still in the shower and Erik disappeared thirty minutes ago, saying he needed to grab some stuff."

Maggie sat in the overstuffed chair in the corner of the enormous suite. There was a wet bar behind her, a comfortable sofa facing a massive wall-mounted TV and an office studio off to the side. "I can't believe they put us in a five-star hotel in Dawson City. I've never experienced the kind of luxury we've had for the past three days."

Jared raised a brow. "What? Just 'cause we're wolves

doesn't mean we don't know how to behave in high society." He straightened the collar of his white shirt and pulled on a suit jacket. Maggie admired the results. The boy was a walking advertisement for GQ, wolf style. "Damn, can you help me with this? I can never get it straight."

She slapped his hands out of the way to work on his tie. "Staying here is just such a contrast. They start us out with a hike through the wilderness, throw us in the Yukon River and then plant us in Dawson to cool our heels? I mean I've loved the sightseeing and the sleeping in a real bed. And the food...oh my Lord, I've gained ten pounds." She shrugged. "I thought they would make us head right away for the next challenge."

He stepped back to check himself in the mirror. "Remember these Games are supposed to be like the wolf equivalent of the Olympics. Yeah, we all want to do our best, but there's also the good-will-between-packs part. It's a chance to show we can be together without starting territory wars like in the old days."

Maggie collapsed back into the chair. "Jared...I'm going to confess. You guys from the Granite pack are not like any wolves I've met before."

TJ leapt out of the bathroom, stark naked, dripping wet and singing into a hairbrush at the top of his lungs. Jared eyed him for a moment before turning to face Maggie, one brow lifted high. "You were saying?"

She burst out laughing. Jared joined her and the two of them gasped for air as TJ stood in the middle of the room, a confused expression on his face.

"What?"

The main door opened and Erik wandered in, checking out TJ as he paced around him. "Interesting attire. I take it you're going for the super formal look."

"Ha, ha." TJ dragged a towel over his body and nodded at

Erik in his jeans and T-shirt. "What's with you? That's not your usual black-tie outfit."

"Nope."

Maggie rose to examine Erik more closely. The past couple of days he'd been by her side all day long, taking her on tours, buying her trinkets at the souvenir shops. Guarding her when too many wolves crowded around. Then he would kiss her good night outside her hotel room and leave her. Leave her aching and wanting, and she was so ready to rip the clothes right off his gladiator-sized body here and now to sate the urges pulsing through her.

This mate thing was getting seriously out of control.

He winked. "I thought Maggie and I would skip the formal dinner. You two go as the representatives from Granite Lake."

Relief flooded her, the tension headache at the back of her neck slipping away in one smooth stroke. "You mean it?"

He gestured to the basket he'd dropped on the coffee table. "I raided the kitchen. Private picnic for two sound good?"

She threw herself into his arms and buried her face in his neck. She breathed in deeply, his scent filling her head and calming her nerves.

"Thank you," she whispered. He'd known. He'd understood she still couldn't do the whole room full of strange wolves.

Someone cleared their throat and she realized she was not only clinging to Erik, she'd wrapped her legs around his waist and they were rather intimately pressed together. Not that she was embarrassed—wolves were pretty upfront about sex—but if she didn't move soon, they'd be putting on a show, and she really wanted to be alone with him.

Erik lowered her carefully, brushing his knuckles against her cheek before taking her by the hand. "Boys, I expect you to be on your best behaviour. I don't want to be called back to Diamond Tooth Gertie's and find out you've been fighting."

Jared winked. "Tonight, I'm a lover, not a fighter." He turned to TJ. "Did you see the chick on the Norwegian Team? Arwhoo. I claim dibs on that one."

Maggie held on tightly to Erik as he whisked her out of the room and down the ornately decorated hallway. "Are we going to get in trouble for not attending?"

He shook his head. "It's an optional event. The guys will have a good time, there will be a lot of sex happening in the corners of the room, and one team will get thrown out for trying to start a rumble. The usual when you get a big gathering of wolves together."

Oh Lord, now she was even happier she didn't have to attend.

They walked quietly down the historic wooden boardwalk, Maggie pulling in long slow breaths of the fresh air. Above them the sky remained daylight bright.

Erik noticed her gazing upward. "We've traveled far enough north sunset won't happen until just after midnight."

She nodded. "I've missed this part of the North. Before we moved away from Whitehorse I used to love staying up late and going for runs..."

Her throat choked tight and he squeezed her fingers. He led her into the trees and up a narrow path. By the time they broke out above the city, she could breathe again. She stood looking down at the narrow streets nestled against the Yukon River, the hills on the other side still showing their scars from the years of dredge mining. The massive machines had followed the hand miners, scooping up layers of rock and soil to shift out every bit of gold, leaving chunks of broken rubble in their wake.

That was her.

Scarred. Beaten, and pulled apart until there was nothing left of value. At least, that's what she'd felt like before meeting Erik. She sighed. If only it was as easy as bulldozing the rocks aside and planting flowers to cover the scars on her heart.

Erik wrapped his arms around her from the back, pulling her against his warm body. "We need to deal with this tonight. I'm pretty sure the next challenge is going to involve us having to shift. We need to talk."

Anger flared. "This is about me being able to shift? For the Games?" She would have torn herself from his grasp, but suddenly iron bands held her in place.

"Don't. I know you're scared, but don't deliberately try to turn this into a fight to avoid talking to me. I've given you time and space. I just want what's best for you and I don't give a shit if you ever change into a wolf."

He spun her around and clasped her chin, his dark eyes searching hers intently. "I refuse to stand by and let you face tomorrow unprepared. If I'm right, there will be dozens of wolves surrounding you. I won't allow you to walk into that kind of a situation without me trying to take away a little of your fears. You've asked me to wait before joining with you and even though it's been hell, I've waited. But don't ask me to not be your mate, not protect you when I can. Because I won't do it. My wolf won't let me and neither will my human morals."

She stared at him, her limbs trembling as she realized for the first time she was with someone stronger than her who she could really trust. The ache in her soul urged her on.

"You won't tell Missy?"

He jerked back in surprise. "Doesn't she know?"

She shook her head. "She knows parts, but..." Shame covered her. Her own sister had suffered because of Maggie's weakness.

He spread out the blanket he'd brought, sat and pulled her into his lap. Resting her head against his chest, not looking into his eyes, made it easier to speak. She thought for a moment, then simply told her story.

"I don't know why we moved away from Whitehorse. Mom and Dad died before I got a real answer out of them, but Missy and I always suspected it had something to do with our new Alpha in Whistler. He found out something he held over Dad's head to make him move. Once we were in the pack at Whistler, there was no escape for any of us."

She swallowed hard. "The summer I was seventeen, Missy turned twenty-one. Our Alpha wanted her to marry his brother. He was trying to gain control of her Omega skills, but we didn't know it at the time. Missy only knew Jeff wasn't her mate and she refused. So they..." She shivered and burrowed deeper into his arms as if his presence could protect her from the memories.

"They came after you?"

She nodded. "I ran. I hid as a human and when they found me, I shifted and ran again. There were six or seven of them and every time I shifted there was someone in that form to torment me. They hit me." Her voice broke. "They hurt me."

His body tightened under her, indignation and anger pouring off him and forming a protective wall around them. Nothing could touch her right now. He stroked her hair silently for a moment, his heart pounding under her ear.

"Did they rape you?" He spoke softly, gently.

"I don't know!" She squirmed her way back to stare at him. "It sounds so stupid, but I really don't remember. I can feel them grabbing me—my human body—and throwing me on the floor. I shifted, and then there were wolves on top of me, trying to mount me. I shifted back and they tore my skin." She lifted her blouse and twisted to show him the scars along her lower back and her hips. "I shifted so many times in a short period of time I passed out, exhausted from the effort. The next thing I remember is being at home in bed, and Missy telling me she was engaged to Jeff. Dad had made promises to the Alpha and she was furious. I never said a word, but I know it was my fault she ended up in that marriage. Dad sold her off to save me."

She thought she'd already wept all the tears possible over this. Thought the well had run dry and she had nothing left but a cold stone for a heart. But in Erik's arms, his scent surrounding her, she found sorrows she'd never realized she still clung to. Great racking sobs shook her until she was gasping for air.

Erik rocked her, cradled her, his presence embracing her even closer than his arms. He poured love over her, acceptance. His anger simmering underneath didn't frighten her. It reassured her she would never, ever have to face a situation like that again.

When she could speak there was a quiver in her voice. "I left right afterward and never went back. I worked summers and attended UBC and I never shifted into a wolf. Missy and I kept in touch via email and phone, especially after Mom and Dad died in a car accident, but I refused to physically go back to Whistler. Every now and then I'd see pack members hanging around outside my classes, like they were keeping track of me." She shuddered. "Once, they tried to get into the apartment I shared with Pam, but I told her they were cousins I didn't want to see, and somehow she got rid of them."

"I knew I liked her for a reason."

She snorted, and wiped at her teary eyes. "Yeah, well, she thinks you're a little freaky. You know, she's about the best friend I've ever had. Brave and loyal, and fearless and fun, all at the same time. So often I wanted to tell her about being a wolf but I couldn't. I couldn't risk her leaving me."

Erik handed her a hanky and she wiped her face clean. She settled back into his arms, his comfort healing her pain. They sat together for a long time, Erik rubbing her back and whispering foreign phrases to her. She had no idea what he was saying, but the words soothed her, eased the ragged edges around her heart.

"I can see why being around wolves frightens you. Not only was your Alpha a rotten bastard, the whole pack was diseased."

Maggie ran a hand up his forearm to caress his biceps. Touching him made her feel so much better. "I'm surprised you're not offering to go rip out their throats."

"Oh, I'm thinking about it. But your brother-in-law, Tad, already killed the Alpha who instigated the whole thing. What I plan in retaliation for the others' sins you don't have to know about."

She sat up quickly. "You're not going after them."

"They hurt you, you're my mate. There will be an accounting."

"I didn't tell you this so you'd go off half-cocked killing people."

Erik raised a brow. "Killing them. Okay, I had other things in mind, but now you mention it—"

"Stop it. It happened a long time ago. It's been seven years."

"Yet you're still hurting. Sounds like I have cause to give them pain."

She opened her mouth to speak and then froze. Oh damn it. *Damn, damn, damn.*

He was right.

Maggie scrambled out of his lap and stared down at his

dark eyes in horror. A light bulb went on in her head and she could clearly see herself in the room again, the wolves still attacking her. It was like she'd locked the door and never let them go.

She paced toward the nearby trees, grappling with the revelation. She'd suffered years of mental pain and confusion. Loneliness like only a pack animal separated from family could experience. Even the physical weakness caused by locking her wolf away—none of it had been necessary.

She turned to face him. Her gentle giant, staring back with love in his eyes, concern and anger warring in his heart. He'd seen clearly so many times in the past days exactly what she needed. Was it the mate connection that made him able to cut down the walls and help her break free?

Suddenly she knew part of what she needed.

Him.

Two steps forward returned her to where he sat. "This isn't about them, it's me." He moved to speak and she held up her hand. "No, wait and listen. It's true, I'm still in pain. I deliberately didn't see any wolves for years. I didn't visit with my sister in person, and I haven't been able to shift to my wolf in forever. They stole a part of me away and I let them. Ah shit, I let them."

"Maggie...no, don't blame yourself. They were the ones who were wrong. You did nothing to deserve this."

She shook her head. "Don't you see? That's what I'm saying, I felt like I *did* deserve it. It was my fault Missy was trapped, so I let my wolf become trapped as well in punishment. Oh hell, I've been so stupid."

Erik closed his eyes and she felt the rush of his power flow over her. She gasped at the depth of it, the richness of the sensation soaking into her very pores. When he opened his eyes he held out his hand and she grabbed it like a lifeline. "Maggie, I don't know what to say. My brilliant plan to show you my wolf and try to ease your fears seems trite and childish as a solution.

"I feel the strength inside you. Your wolf is powerful and she wants to help you through this. Your heart is so strong, but you've been using your strength to carry a burden that wasn't yours. I meant what I said about not caring if you shift. Only I'd hate to see her trapped forever when together you can be happy again. Truly happy."

"So if tomorrow is a wolf-only challenge, what would you do?"

He shrugged. "As far as I'm concerned we can go home. This is a game, what you're talking about is real life."

Maggie shook her head. "No! If we go home that's another thing they've stolen from me. From the boys, and the pack. No more. I've had enough of them taking my life away. I want to compete and I want to get my life back on track." Tears filled her eyes again. She dropped to her knees at his feet and clasped his big hands in hers. "Help me."

Erik rubbed his thumb over her knuckles. "I agree you need to take back control of your life, but Maggie..." He cupped her face in his hand. "You've *been* reclaiming your life. Ever since you started back north you've taken charge and made changes. If you can't finish it all in a few days, you're still well on the way. They aren't winning anymore. You're the one in control of the game now. Okay?"

Her heart leapt. It was true. She nodded jerkily.

"Summer solstice is tomorrow. I think that should help." He pulled off his shirt and her mouth watered. Firm muscles tempted her. Distracted her from the emotional rollercoaster she'd just raced over. The urgent desire to run her tongue over his body chased away all other thoughts. How had they resisted completing their mating until now? It was another stone to cast at the feet of her tormentors. Then he was naked, every glorious mile of him spread out like a banquet before her.

"I have no idea how this is supposed to help my wolf, but damn you're fine."

He laughed. "You're drooling."

She wiped at her mouth in response and flushed when he laughed again. "Tease."

"I like the look in your eyes."

Maggie lifted her gaze to his. "You're much better looking than TJ. At least to me."

Erik patted the blanket beside him. "I thought I'd change to my wolf, but I want you to be sure you understand it's me, no matter what form I take. If I frighten you, just tell me to shift back and I will."

"I've been around TJ's wolf for three days."

He frowned. "Sweetheart, I hate to remind you, but TJ is young and not as powerful as you. He's also not nearly as big as I am. When we do have a shifter challenge there will be few wolves my size. If you can get comfortable around me, that's the first step."

Maggie nodded. "Makes sense."

"Touch me."

She ran her hands up his chest, over all that hard muscle and tight skin, leaning closer to brush their lips together. The thrill of connection shook her to the core even as their lips stayed soft and sweet. She took her time, tracing the tattoos on his shoulders and arms, brushing the stiff hair on his head. She stroked her hands down his abdomen, skirting his erection.

Oh heavens. Distraction at its very finest.

"I think I should shift now."

She nodded, unable to tear her eyes away from the evidence of just how much he really wanted her.

"Maggie, did you hear me? I'm going to shift." A tug on her arm made her drag her gaze back to his face. Erik wore a huge grin. "Although that's a very nice expression you've got right now."

"Okay, Wolfman, let me clap for you."

Shimmering light flashed, transposing images registered on her retinas, and Erik lay on the blanket, all claws and black fur and teeth, and for one awful second, her heart stopped. She closed her eyes and felt for him. It was still Erik. Still the same sensation of power rolling off him, the same love and caring being projected. Gentleness mixed with his incredible strength.

Between the two of them, there was nothing they couldn't accomplish.

Suddenly, that was all she needed. The final wall fell.

"Shift. I need to...I want to..."

She waited, shaking with the fever rippling through her veins. Her blouse came off in one motion, her skirt and bits of underwear flying after it. He changed back, his solid body reforming until he lay on the blanket, naked. She leapt on him, into his arms, tears pouring from her eyes.

"What's wrong? I'm sorry, I didn't mean to push you too fast. You don't have to change. Maggie? Why are you naked?"

She sealed her mouth to his, stealing his words, taking his response. She lay skin-to-skin on top of him, his erection pressing against her belly. She wanted him. Needed him desperately, and there was nothing that would stop her.

He rolled them over, pausing before he covered her. He tangled his fingers in her hair, his tongue stroking and dancing with hers. The wind rustled the leaves overhead, swirls of his power wrapping around them. The pulsing beat between her legs jumped in tempo when he dragged a hand down her body and cupped her breast in the palm of his hand.

When he pulled back they both gasped for air. He stroked his thumb around the tender skin of her nipple, circling again and again as he stared into her eyes. "Are you sure? Make no mistake, I love you and I want you, but I will wait until you're really ready. Don't do this to try and convince your wolf to rise. Don't do this unless you mean it."

Maggie brought her hands to cradle his face. He was so damn big it was easy to forget just how tenderhearted he really was. Her wolf danced inside, waiting to be set free. But before she let her out, she wanted to please the woman.

"The mate thing? It's there, I feel the chemistry between us. But my head says I love you as well. My wolf loves you. And now we need to stop talking and I need you inside me. Please."

He closed his eyes, his face tight with restrained desire. "I didn't want this to happen here. In the wilderness, no soft bed. I wanted it to be special."

She slapped his shoulder. "Damn, it is special. It's you, and me and that's—"

He leaned over to consume her.

Chapter Ten

Soft warm skin under his mouth, her scent filling his head. If he never saw another sunrise, just the memory of this moment—his mate accepting him—would keep him warm for the rest of his life.

She caressed his body, her hands tiny against his chest, over his shoulders. Her touch teased and tormented and he slipped a line of kisses down her torso, partly in an attempt to escape to where he could concentrate on her without being distracted. He cupped her breasts in his hands, the dark skin of her nipples crinkling tight as he lapped at them. First one then the other, licking and nipping and sucking until Maggie panted and writhed under him.

"I love the way you taste." He licked her belly button and she laughed, her torso shaking.

"You talk too much."

"Hmm, you think?"

"Oh. Oh. Oh yes..."

Erik smiled against her core, his tongue tracing lazy circles around the rigid nub of her clitoris. He continued his assault, his tongue and fingers playing her like an instrument, now fast, now slower. The sounds of delight she made changed with his tempo until she tightened around his fingers, her sheath squeezing the two fingers he'd buried in her depths.

Again and again he lapped at her, lifting her hips high in the air to pull her closer to his eager mouth. The connection between them grew stronger the longer they touched, and the control he'd wound up, tight as a corkscrew, slowly began to unravel. Destiny meant for them to be together, but after hearing her confession he admired her more than ever. She was brave and bright, and she drove him totally and completely mad with lust.

"Erik!"

He stilled his hand where he'd reached under her hips to caress the tight star of her anus. A light sheer of sweat broke out on her skin and as she lay before him, her body shaking with another orgasm, he'd never seen a more beautiful sight.

"I love you." He lowered her hips to the blanket and crawled over her, needing to taste her lips again. She clung to his neck and attempted to pull their bodies together. He laughed against her mouth, unwilling to crush her with his weight. She arched under him, rubbing their torsos together, stoking his fires hotter. Moisture from her crotch painted his skin and he groaned. *Gotta keep it slow.* No matter how much he wanted to thrust into her, bury himself in her sweetness. He kissed her, anchored on his elbows to keep them apart.

Maggie poked him in the ribs. "You're too big."

"I'm not even touching you yet."

She laughed with delight and pushed him until he sat up. "Nothing wrong with your ego, is there?" She straddled his thighs, her breasts crushed against his chest, the heat of her pussy now lined up properly with his aching shaft. "Missy wondered if we'd have to—"

"I really don't want to talk about your sister right now. Oh damn, Maggie."

She'd maneuvered herself over the crown of his cock and

slowly rode him. Each movement of her hips brought him farther into her body, the tight clasp of her sheath wrapping around him like a bit of heaven. He supported her hips and helped her, watching her face carefully. She kissed his chest as she settled, his entire length buried inside. "You feel so good in me."

He linked his fingers in her hair, tugging her gaze up to his. "Together. Like we were meant to be."

A mischievous smile crossed her face and she grabbed his shoulders, lifting her hips high until his cock clung to her opening. She dropped down, smooth and fast, hard and amazing. Electric tingles started in his spine and spread fingers out to his balls. There was no way he was going to last. Not after waiting almost two weeks, wanting her desperately the whole time.

She rubbed herself against him on every motion, their bodies slick in the heat of the night. The expression on her face fascinated him and he stared as he assisted her sweet assault on his cock. She bit her bottom lip, her breath coming out in panting gasps.

"More. I want more." Her thoughts sounded in his mind and he hummed with delight.

Tendrils of knowledge twined from her around his heart—the sensations she felt, the emotions racing through her—all of it passing between them as their mate connection bound them together. He reached out to share his love, his passion for her. How proud he was of her strength. How touched at her willingness to trust him. Their bodies meshed as their minds linked.

She cried out, coming around him, and he let go of his control. Locked together they both reveled in the exquisite explosion. He held her close as after-tremors shook her, the heat of their bodies spreading like a cocoon around them.

"Erik? Is it really happening?"

"Oh yeah, sweetheart. It's real and it's right." He brushed a curl back from her face, leaning closer to kiss her again. The sense of completeness was so amazing. All the missing parts of his soul settled into place as both memories of the past and dreams for the future passed between them.

The mate connection—linking them together intimately. Everything he'd longed for to make him complete, and it had finally happened. He kissed her without stopping, the need to show her his total love and commitment overwhelming him. She smiled against his lips, their tongues dancing together, a sweet and content exploration now that the fire had flared.

"I love you." He kissed her eyelids and the tip of her nose, and she laughed out loud.

"You talk too much."

He laughed, stroking her back, enjoying the way she nestled against him, warm and satisfied.

"Erik? I love you too."

How could feeling so wonderful make his heart ache?

His anger at what she'd experienced continued to simmer. It would be a long time before he'd be able to forget how broken she'd been by the attack. Her power as a wolf slipped up a notch and she twisted in his arms. She stared at him, determination written all over her face.

He sent her acceptance for who she was, what she was, not only to him but the pack as well. *"You don't have to do this yet."*

She raised a brow. "Scared she's going to outrun you?"

He felt it. As she reached down deep and called up her wolf, joy overflowed her heart. Aching loneliness from being forced down for so many years washed away. Maggie backed from him, her bright eyes watching closely.

"I'm glad you're here. I'm glad we're together for this." As she reached her hands to the sky, a beam of midnight sun broke through the trees to set her skin glowing. She shifted, shimmered, and Erik knelt forward to rejoice as she paced over to him in wolf, her silvery coat gleaming with health. She leaned forward, her tail wagging with delight and he laughed out loud.

"Shall we run, my mate?" Maggie bumped him with her head, wrapping herself around his torso.

He shifted, his wolf eager to meet his counterpart. They stood nose to nose for moment, sharing their hearts in wolf form. Erik took off at a run, letting Maggie follow him until they reached the far side of the hill. He stepped aside and she took the lead, her joy in her wolf trailing behind her like a bright rainbow.

He threw back his head and howled, letting the whole world know. He had his mate, they were together. Life couldn't get much better than this.

"I can't believe it. You hadn't shifted for seven years? Damn. Someone needs their butts whooped." Jared glared into the distance and TJ growled in agreement.

Maggie held up a hand. "Guys. Put your testosterone back in your pants. I didn't tell you about my issue to get you riled up." She leaned back on Erik's sturdy frame as she faced TJ and Jared. Both the young men's wolves hovered just under the surface, furious for her sake. She tested her fear at the proximity of more wolves, but there was nothing there. Just calm reassurance emanating from Erik like a lifeline. Craning her head back, she blew him a kiss. *"Thank you for letting me do this my way."*

"Sure, but you'd better finish before they shift without meaning to. Jared especially is really pissed off. You've got an admirer I need to worry about?"

She nudged him in the gut. "I thought you boys needed to know. Last night I shifted, and it was glorious. There will be no troubles in the challenge with me running, but I still don't know how I'll feel when faced with a bunch of strange wolves. I don't want you to get upset if I freak out. With the mate connection between me and Erik, I think I have the strength, but you're my pack now too, and I'm trusting you to help me."

TJ grinned at Jared. "I told you so."

"Yeah, yeah. Mr. Sniffy and his Magic Nose have spoken. Hey, congrats on the mate thing." Jared winked at her before breaking into a huge yawn.

She laughed. "I take it you had a good time last night with Miss Norway?"

Jared glared at TJ who shuffled off a few feet. "Well one of us had a good time."

Laughter rumbled against her back. "TJ? You stole Jared's woman? Again?"

Maggie choked. "TJ?"

He managed to look guilty. He shrugged. "Can I help it if the girls all love the underdog?"

A loud bell rang in the distance.

Erik squeezed her for a second before letting go. "There's the call. Leave everything in the room. They said they'd shuttle us back here when the event is done."

They were all gathered at the starting line. Maggie kept Erik between her and the rest of the crowd without even thinking about it. After so many years of avoidance, she wasn't going to be able to change habits overnight. She took a deliberate step forward and caught Erik grinning down at her.

"Well done, love."

She lifted her chin a little higher and turned to listen to the Games Marshal.

"We're starting the event here instead of in town for the sake of the humans. We'd like to thank all of you for the restraint you showed last night while in Dawson. There were only a few comments this morning at the local coffee shops about unusual wolf sightings, so you seem to have managed to keep yourselves under control while in range of cell phones and other recording devices."

Jared nudged TJ and the two of them snickered.

"What do you think that's about?" Maggie asked.

"I really don't think I want to know."

"Today's challenge is a foot race. Cross country toward the Dempster Highway. We've got a loop through the Tombstone Mountains, finishing at the Tombstone campground. All the campers are ours, and we've closed the area to hunting for safety's sake. It's an all-out sprint for your wolves. No bonus points available. At the end of this event, we'll calculate the scores and announce the current standings. Final event will be held in two days' time."

All around them teams were stripping and shifting. Maggie watched in morbid fascination, wondering when the sense of utter horror would creep up her spine and throttle her.

It never came. They were only wolves.

She walked boldly toward the nearest team, shaking off Erik's hand. "I need to do this."

Her opponents watched her warily as she stepped into their

midst and stood there.

Nothing. They were only...wolves.

She threw back her head and laughed, joy springing up again.

"You want to come and join us, love? I think you're freaking out our opponents and that's not very sportsmanlike."

Oh shit. She bowed politely to the captain of the team, backing away with deference before leaping into Erik's arms. "I can do this. I really and truly can do this."

He patted her cheek. "I knew you could. Now get naked, little wolf, and let's go for a run."

Stripping off her clothes was freeing. Seeing the admiration in her mate's eyes brought even more pleasure. But the sensation of shifting itself was almost orgasmic. Last night she'd been too worried she wouldn't be able to shift, she'd missed the awesome physical rush. Today she experienced it fully, moaning with delight.

"Are you going to do that every time you shift? Because, holy shit, that was hot..." Erik nudged her flank and her wolf took control, teasing and rubbing against her mate. *"Whoa, sweetheart. We're in the middle of a contest. Remember? As much as I enjoy sex with you, now is not the time. Rein her in."*

Maggie dropped her haunches to sit on the grass. TJ and Jared sniffed her before rolling and offering their throats in submission. If there had been time, she would have howled with delight.

The gun went off and they were away, racing shoulder by shoulder through the Yukon scrub. Brush that was thigh high on a human was level with her head, and she trusted Erik and the others as taller wolves to choose the most direct path through the maze of tough tangle.

Suddenly they broke out into the clear, the sky overhead bright blue, not a cloud to be seen. They ran. Side by side, paws and legs flying, heads and torsos almost touching they were so close together.

There was something wonderful in the freedom of running with a pack again. While last night with Erik had been amazing, today was an answer to another part of the puzzle she'd been missing forever. Belonging. Connecting. A part of a greater whole. Maggie's heart pounded in time with their paws on the ground, eating up the miles. Ahead she scented the trail they followed. The more time passed, the clearer it became, almost as if the years of being trapped fell away and musty cobwebs brushed from the corners of her wolf's mind.

They tore down a hill and splashed through a stream at the widest point, spray rising and soaking their fur. The fresh, crisp air and the bright green growth teased and inspired her senses to greater heights. Ahead, Erik led the way.

Her mate.

Her heart.

She nuzzled his flank with her nose and thrilled at the connection between them. TJ and Jared fell back slightly, letting her and Erik lead, and the moment became even more incredible.

"You're running well."

"I'm alive. Truly alive." It was all she had to say and it meant the world.

They must have run for an hour before the trail veered to the side, upward, forcing them to push harder as they topped the mountainside. Now there were large boulders blocking their way and the trail grew narrower. The teams of wolves joined together, forced by the narrowing path to fight for dominance. Maggie stuck close to Erik, her heart beating faster as snarls and the clash of teeth rose behind her.

Erik maneuvered her to his left. TJ growled and there was a yipping cry. She glanced over her shoulder to see four large wolves closing in. Jared and TJ had been separated from them, and a raw slash showed on Jared's shoulder.

"Erik?"

"It's the cheaters from the river. Darren never was one to learn easily. Do you mind if I teach him a lesson?" Fear skittered across her mind, her throat tightening. Darren. The one who'd leered at her. Then Erik's will soothed her, strengthened her. *"It's not a challenge to the death, but if I don't do something, who will?"*

That was Erik to a fault. How could she not agree when his sense of fair play and justice was so much a part of who he was? She took a centering breath and reluctantly agreed.

The power within Erik snapped like a live wire, hot and out of control. He turned in one smooth motion and barreled into the leader of the other foursome. They rolled together, stopping with Erik pinning the other wolf to the ground under him. He held Darren by the throat, growling in triumph.

"That was quick."

"Bullies are usually wimps."

A low rumble to her right brought Maggie's attention snapping back. Two of the wolves from the other team surrounded her, their lips curled to show their bared canines. Her knees went weak as memories rushed over her. Growls and tearing pain, sleepless nights and nightmares. She wavered for a second.

"Maggie, fight back. You're strong, there is nothing they can do to you."

One of the wolves snapped at her hind leg and she whirled

on him. Pulling herself to her full height, she let her anger and frustration at being cowed rise. Too many years. She'd had too many years of being the one to run and hide, and she wasn't going to do it again. A scary growling filled her ears, startling her for a moment until she realized it was her making the racket.

She stared the wolf down, pacing forward deliberately. He retreated, swinging his head to the side, looking for his backup. Maggie lunged at him, batting at his head with the back of her paw. She didn't want to draw blood, just make him stop. How dare this team turn what was supposed to be a fun event into something fearful? Inside her, anger continued to build. It exploded out, her power flying in his face. He dropped to his belly in an instant and cowered in submission. Turning to face the other wolf, she discovered he'd disappeared under TJ and Jared. Erik howled once, a long low cry that filled the mountaintop with his power. Darren sulked off as Erik rose to stride toward her. Jared licked at his shoulder and she joined him, knocking him to the ground with her body so she could look over the wound. The scratch wasn't too bad, so she let him up, reassuring him with a touch of her nose to his chin.

Erik stroked her muzzle with his. *"Thank you, Beta, for helping care for our pack."*

The lump in her throat felt very strange in wolf form. *"Shit."*

He gave a wolfie chuckle. *"You just realized that now? Yup. You and me, second in command. So what do you say we get running? No one else is going through the pass until we get started and if we sit here too long the people at the finish area are going to wonder what's happened."*

She remained immobile, confused by his words. *"No one else?"*

He bumped her gently, turning her to face down the hillside

they'd ascended before the attack. The rest of the competitors lay huddled in groups on the rocky ground, all eyes watching them intently. Darren and his team sat forlornly at the extreme edge of the gathering, dust covered and looking whipped.

She considered for a moment. *"Are they waiting for us to go first?"*

TJ's tail beat the ground so hard dust swirled into the air around them, and Erik nudged him to get him to stop. Maggie threw back her head and howled with delight. Her wolf was awake, she was whole again, and she and her team had just been honoured by an entire group of wolves.

When the echoes of the all the responding cries stopped ringing off the sheer rock cliffs around them, she rose, Erik and the boys joining her. They turned and ran, following the trail to the finish line.

Maggie couldn't care less about the Games. She'd already won the greatest prize imaginable, and he ran beside her all the way.

Epilogue

"I can't believe you guys got disqualified from the final event. You were in second place headed into it." Keil sighed in disgust. They sat on the front porch of Tad's house, watching Jared and TJ out on the front lawn arguing as Jared hobbled around on crutches.

Erik laughed. "There's something in the rules that says competitors with broken legs are not eligible, no matter how fast we heal. When the idiot got hit by a car while gawking at the ladies en route to the challenge, there was no way to explain to the human authorities Jared didn't need to go to the hospital. It's okay, everyone was impressed we had the most clues after acing the Peter-and-wolf thing. We also got awarded the trophy for most sportsmanlike team."

"It's a damn big trophy—looks great in the pack house. The old timers were thrilled to see it."

Tad drove up and rolled down his window. "Have you guys seen Jamie? Missy wants me to bring him to the hospital to meet the babies."

Erik rose from his chair. "I think he's with Maggie in the kitchen. I'll go get them."

He rounded the corner, following the invisible connection he had with his mate. The sensation made him smile. He always knew where she was, but more importantly, now she knew she was right where she was supposed to be.

With him.

They still had to figure out where they were going to live until they built their house, but the satisfaction of making those decisions together met a great need in him.

Jamie raced past, his fat little legs pumping wildly.

"You can outrun your mama, but you can't outrun me." Maggie scooped up the squealing toddler, tossing him into the air before catching him and tickling him. His laughter filled the room.

Erik leaned against the wall, soaking it all in.

She glanced at him, her eyes bright with love. "I knew you were there."

"Unca Eri." Jamie squealed louder. He squirmed out of her arms and attacked Erik's leg, his pudgy fingers grasping the cotton fabric of his pants leaving sticky smears behind. Maggie giggled behind her hand as he picked the little tyke up and tickled him under the chin.

Erik beamed at her. "You want to go visit Missy and the girls again? Tad's taking Jamie."

Maggie raised her brows. "Hmm, that means the place will be empty." She winked at him. "I'm thinking I should stay here, just in case anyone needs something. I can...guard the house."

"Oh." He transferred the toddler to his other arm and held out his hand to her. She cuddled in close, rubbing against his chest. "Do you need a hand? The guarding? I think it's a big house, with lots of bedrooms."

"Uh-huh. I could use a little backup."

They grinned at each other.

Erik cleared his throat. "By the way. Pam left another bunch of phone messages for you. You'd better call her soon and let her know we didn't bury your body in the bush."

Maggie laughed. "You really okay with us inviting her to the wedding? It's going to make things awkward, since no one will be able to shift while she's around."

He shrugged. "We'll have two ceremonies. The second after she leaves will be the one with naked wolves roaming the halls of the pack house. In the meantime..." He squeezed her tight for a second, adjusted little Jamie in his arms, and led them off in search of Tad. "We have someone to deliver to his daddy, and then you and I, little wolf, have a date."

She tugged his hand until he bent over far enough for her to press a kiss on his cheek. "I love you. I'm so glad I was brave enough to come north again."

"I love you too. You're brave enough to face a whole pack of wolves. Even one as big as me."

Wolf Tracks

Dedication

This one's for you—the readers. From Molli, who's been begging for TJ's story since day one, to the woman who emailed to tell me she read the whole series back to back over a weekend. You are why this story was even written. Thank you for taking the wolfies and giving them so much loving.

Arwhooooo.

Chapter One

Pam let out a long, slow whistle and stared out the window to admire the scenery one more time. "Damn it, Maggie, I knew you were hiding something, but seriously. How many can I take home?"

A light tap on her arm dragged her attention away from the backyard and the succulent array of man flesh congregating there. "You're supposed to be helping me, not drooling over the wedding guests." Maggie turned her back and gestured over her shoulder. "Get the last of my buttons, will you?"

"Where did you get this gorgeous gown so quickly up here in the boonies? I mean, it's been two months since you went north. Not that I've been calculating or anything, but sixty-seven days is a short time to fall in love, get engaged and arrange to tie the knot." Pam slipped the last of the minuscule pearl buttons through the hoops. Two months since she'd seen her friend, and falling in love didn't seem to be the only thing that had changed. Pam checked the bedroom they were in with a growing suspicion Maggie was keeping secrets from her. Something wasn't sitting right, and over the years Pam had learned to trust her instincts.

"It's my sister's dress. I just had to add a little bit of lace to the bottom to deal with the difference in our heights." Maggie twirled, the lacey layers of the skirt flying around her. Her short blonde curls bounced more wildly than usual, a thin silver tiara nestled amidst the chaos. "How do I look?"

Pam rolled her eyes. "Like a freaking pixie queen, as usual. God, why do you even ask? You'd be gorgeous in a paper bag."

Maggie laughed.

It was now or never. "I need to know, Mags. Is this really something you want to do? Or are you getting married this fast because, oh, you feel you have to..."

Her best friend frowned. "Do you think I'm being forced into this? Seriously, I'm in love and I want to marry Erik."

"You're not pregnant and thinking this is the only way to deal with it, 'cause, if you are, I'd be totally fine with helping support you—"

"Pam!" Maggie trapped her in her arms, squeezed with the tightest bear hug possible. "Oh, sweetie, I'm honoured you're willing to help me, but I'm not pregnant. I'm honestly and truly in love. I know it seems fast, but with some...people, you know it's right."

That was possible. Maybe. Pam had rarely seen it. She turned away to stop Maggie from reading her expression too closely. Just because she'd never seen a real-life "love you forever" didn't mean it couldn't happen, and someone's wedding day was hardly the time to point that out. She sighed and tried to distract herself with the man candy again. "So. When you and Erik take off on your honeymoon, do I get to sample the locals?"

Maggie's laugh tickled her ears and then everything was okay again. "You're such a flirt. Go easy on them, heartbreaker. Hey, I need a few minutes alone. Why don't you go explore? Come back in about twenty and I'll be ready to roll."

Pam kissed her cheek. "If you're sure you're sure."

"God, go on. I'm a big girl now." They grinned at each other with the familiarity of long-time friends before Pam scooted downstairs. She peeked into the bustling kitchen before wandering out into the yard.

"Hey, can I get you a drink?"

"Are you hungry?"

Suddenly surrounded by tall men in formal suits, her mouth watered. Another voice lifted over the others and a light touch landed on her shoulder.

"Here. For you." A Gerard Butler look-alike offered her a glass of white wine. She shook her head. Did they think she just fell off the turnip truck? She didn't take drinks from strange men, even drool-worthy ones.

"You're Maggie's friend, right?"

"Would you like to go for a walk for a few minutes? I can show you around the yard."

One of them offered his elbow and she batted her lashes as she took it. Why not? She had time before Maggie wanted her back. A couple of children raced past their feet and Pam smiled as she watched the happy chaos filling the festively decorated yard. "Nice crowd for the wedding. Do all you boys live around here?"

It had been awhile since she'd had such tasty company, let alone this many good-looking guys. While the attention was diverting, she wasn't in the market for a relationship while she was in the North. Nope. She'd do the "support my friend" thing with Maggie, take off for a little sightseeing, then it was back to civilization all the way. And beautiful men like these—well, a one-night stand would be fun but the bridesmaid getting it on at the wedding was a cliché she really wanted to avoid in this lifetime.

Maggie's fiancé strode over, towering above the other men.

Pam chuckled. While he'd turned out to be one of the good guys, she'd still kick his butt if he needed it, no matter how big he was. No one messed with her friends, and Maggie was her oldest friend. BFF and all that shit.

"You doing okay? The boys treating you right?" Erik glanced around, his expression stern, and the fawning crew raced away like they'd been shot out of a cannon. Pam stared at their retreating backs with growing suspicion. No way. If he'd put them up to it...

"I guess that's the question, isn't it?" She narrowed her eyes. "I was getting the royal treatment. That your doing?"

Erik held up his hands, palms out. "Trust me. I don't feel like having you tear a strip off me. If they're hanging around, it's because you're interesting. Just don't break too many hearts, okay? I'd hate to have to listen to sucky love songs during karaoke night for months after you leave."

Pam laughed. "Okay, you're safe. I believe you." She shook her head as she glanced up and down his length. "What the hell do you guys eat up here? Is there like a fountain of hugeness or something? I've counted at least two dozen men over six-three in height."

He grinned at her. "It's the water. Seriously good. Hey, Maggie says she needs you one last time, but I was hoping to introduce you to my best man first." He glanced around. "Only he seems to have disappeared."

Pam waved a hand at him. "I'll meet him when we do the little walk-thing around the yard. Maggie explained the procedure and I'm cool with the ceremony. I'd better run and see what she wants. Just in case she's getting cold feet and wants me to call the whole thing off on her behalf."

She hid her amusement as his smile drained away. "You don't think she would? But..."

It had taken years to perfect the fake concerned expression she wore as she nodded sympathetically at him. "I'm sure it will be fine, but I'd better go settle her down. You stay here and try not to worry." She patted him on the arm and went back upstairs, snickering evilly.

Maggie met her at the top of the landing. Pam tried to wipe her face clean of her grin, but they'd been best friends for too long.

"Who are you tormenting now? Pam, you promised not to freak people out with your weird sense of humour."

Someone stepped to the side of Maggie. Pam turned to face the young man and stopped dead. *My oh my.* She flushed at the expression in his eyes. The last time a guy had stared at her like that, the two of them had been naked, in the middle of a heated sexual exchange. He stripped her with his gaze and rather than feel indignant, her own interest rose. Of course, he was too young for her, but still... Hot damn, he *was* hot. Darkish skin, black hair. Eyes so black the pupils and irises bled together. That must be it—his pupils—it only looked like he was one step away from ravishing her.

"Pam, I'd like you to meet TJ. He's a good friend and works with Erik as a wilderness guide. He's going to be our best man."

TJ held out his hand, stepping closer, and she forced herself to resist backing away. She grasped his fingers, intending to give him a firm business-like handshake when he flipped her palm down and raised her hand to his mouth. "My pleasure. Really."

He leaned forward and kissed her knuckles. An icy chill slipped up her spine and oh my God, her body grew instantly wet. *Damn!* Did he just lick her skin? She knew she was staring, but there seemed to be no way to tear her gaze from his. Even after he straightened, he refused to let her fingers drop and she stood there like some freaking garden gnome statue with her hand limp-wristed in his, hoping by some weird circumstance they'd magically turn out to be standing alone in a bedroom with a mattress on the firm side bumping the back of her knees. Lust stole her tongue.

"TJ?" Maggie elbowed him and he shook himself, like he was waking up. He took a deep breath and his eyes widened even farther. Pam glanced away, anywhere had to be safer than staring into those fuck-me-now bedroom eyes. Until she noticed she'd lowered her gaze and watched the front of his dress pants tent, his erection growing more and more obvious.

"Pam?" She dragged her gaze up to see Maggie examining her with concern. "I think we need to go downstairs. Right now." Maggie tugged her arm, pulling her toward the top of the stairs and away from the fascinating young man in the tuxedo.

With a deep sense of regret, Pam turned her back on the dark god who watched her with hungry eyes.

Shit.

Shit.

TJ swallowed hard and immediately regretted it. His tongue had picked up the flavour of the woman Maggie had dragged off and now the chemicals once again raced through his body, making him ache.

Shit.

How was it possible? Maggie had pulled him aside to warn him, again, he couldn't let her friend know anything about them being wolves because Pam was full human. He was not to let the werewolf out of the bag, so to speak. He felt a little indignant Maggie treated him like a child and expected him to screw up. Just because he'd accidentally shifted once before. Or twice. But both those instances were years ago. He was twenty-two, and while he still preferred his wolf form for high-dexterity moves, his human was getting better. Besides, Keil had already issued orders in his high and mighty alpha voice for all pack members to remain unfurry for the duration of the wedding. No one would disobey his direct command.

Still...*shit.*

It was a good thing Maggie *had* warned him, because incredibly his first impulse upon laying eyes on the beauty was to shift and bury his nose in her dark brown hair. He wanted to sniff her all over, then change back to human form to lick her, starting at her toes and getting delightfully distracted long before reaching anywhere near her throat.

His cock ached, and his vision blurred. Damn if his hearing wasn't buzzing as well. Suddenly the world began to shake and he wondered how badly he'd lost it before he realized Erik had grabbed him by the arms and stared into his face with concern.

"TJ? What the hell is up? Maggie called me through our mental link and told me to get up here and deal with you. Were you about to shift?"

That settled TJ quickly.

"No!" Crap, not another doubter of his ability to hold it together. Although something was seriously fucked. He sighed. "It's just..."

He closed his eyes and took a deep sniff. Erik's scent was the strongest, followed by Maggie's, but wrapping around them both was a tantalizing and intoxicating aroma that tickled his libido and kicked it into overdrive. "Erik, are we *sure* Pam doesn't have wolf in her bloodline?"

Erik leaned back and crossed his arms. "Positive. Maggie lived with her for years. Both the Omegas have met her and she's pure human. One hundred percent." His gaze narrowed. "What are you not saying?"

TJ wrinkled his nose. "You know how you've always said I've got a keen sense of smell?"

"The best in the pack."

He snorted and shook his head. "Then you'll be pleased to know my awesome sniffer has just told me Maggie's best friend, fully human and not possibly eligible for the honour...is my fucking mate."

Chapter Two

He'd found a new form of hell. TJ paced slowly around the outer edge of the backyard, his freaking mate on his arm and all he could talk about was...nothing. He couldn't tell her he was weak at the knees at the thought of finding her. Couldn't say how important she was to him. He concentrated on keeping his feet on the ground because there was no way he was going to trip and be an ass in front of her.

Erik had made him swear he wouldn't say anything prematurely. Until TJ talked to his brother, the Alpha, chatting up his mate was outlawed, and the kicker was Erik had actually pulled a Beta move and *ordered* TJ to stay quiet. The damn hierarchy of the pack froze his tongue. Now torn between the dire need to haul Pam off somewhere private to bind them together for the rest of their days and the violent need to obey a direct command—TJ was screwed.

He glanced sideways to admire her again. A few dark strands had fallen from the fancy hairdo, framing her face. She smiled at everyone, but the tension in her body screamed at him and all he wanted to do was ease her burden.

"You okay?"

She met his gaze then flushed darker. "How many times do we do this?"

"Walk the loop? Three. You should slow down a bit so we

don't step on Erik's and Maggie's heels." He pulled his elbow in so the back of her fingers touched his ribs. True, there were a few layers of clothing between them, but it was better than nothing.

This was driving him mad. He smelled her skin, the natural perfume of her body. Her arousal. His heart pounded, and he strove to keep his face neutral and not pant like a dog. How everyone around didn't notice they were both leaking mating scents was beyond his comprehension.

Another deep breath made his mouth water and his cock jerk. There was no denying it. It was impossible and it had happened. His one-and-only forever mate was a human.

He was okay with it. It was weird and insane, but since they were mates, there was a reason for it and they'd figure it out. First it seemed he was going to have to not only convince her they belonged together, but the entire leadership of his pack.

Starting with big brother Keil and his mate Robyn. The Alphas of the Granite Lake pack sat in the front row with their little girl perched quietly on Keil's knee. Robyn frowned at TJ, using sign language to unobtrusively ask what was wrong. He shook his head quickly. This wasn't going to be an easy explanation.

Pam unconsciously rubbed her fingers up and down his arm. The slight movement taunted him. Drove him insane. He reached over and placed his other hand on top of hers.

"Don't."

She stiffened in response and tried to pull away. Pain raced through him at having his mate unsure and a little frightened, and suddenly he didn't give a *damn* what his Beta had told him. His tongue loosened, the restriction binding him falling away. He was going to care for her, let her know everything was going to be okay. If he happened to mention he wanted her sometime during the conversation...so be it.

He leaned his head closer, breathing in as much of her scent as possible. "It's okay. You were tickling me. I like you holding me, but the rubbing was distracting."

She stayed silent for a moment then adjusted her grip. "I'm sorry. I didn't mean to."

TJ chuckled. "You're distracting no matter what you're doing." He smiled at her and winked. "I kinda like it."

She frowned. "Like what?"

"Being distracted by you."

She shook her head as they took the corner at the far end of the yard and headed back to the starting position for the second lap. "How old are you?"

He paused. "Why?"

In spite of licking her lips and sending a shot of lust through his core, the expression in her eyes was friendly, not flirtatious. "I don't rob cradles."

Damn it. "I'm legal in all states and provinces."

"You're a baby. Cute, but a baby."

"Is that why you wanted to crawl into bed with me when we met at the top of the stairs?" She stumbled and he caught her quickly. "Shit. Sorry, that wasn't very polite. True, but not very polite."

"I did not want to—"

"Careful. Maggie told me you were the most trustworthy person she'd ever met. Hate to ruin your reputation."

She growled and he grinned. Feisty wench. He liked that in a woman.

"Fine. You're a good-looking guy and yeah, I did picture

tangling the sheets with you." *Hallelujah!* "But you're too young and I'm here for the wedding and that's it."

TJ tried to keep the image of them naked in bed from distracting him as they walked in silence for another few paces. Unfortunately he had a good imagination. The too-young thing he could work around. The fact she was being stubborn? Oh, he loved a challenge.

"Stop it," she whispered. Her voice was deep and husky, slipping like a caress over his already super-sensitive nerves.

"Stop what?"

She wiggled her hand on his arm. "That. You're...rubbing me."

Oops. He stilled his thumb from the circles he was tracing on the back of her hand. Seemed neither of them could resist touching each other, which only made sense as mates. A faint flush covered her soft skin from the low neckline of her dress up to her hairline, and he had to look away before he did something too wolfish like drop her to the ground and lick her until she screamed in pleasure.

"What happens after the ceremony?" Pam asked. "I forgot to check with Maggie to see if there was anything I needed to do."

I take you home and make love to you all night long. "We head in, enjoy dinner then I'm singing before the dance begins."

"You sing?" There was a trace of something in her voice. Doubt?

"I sing. Are you surprised?"

"Not at all," she lied.

TJ snorted. It was a deception he recognized easily. After too many years of being expected to screw things up, he knew exactly what someone meant when they spoke in that particular tone of voice.

"You want to join me for a few songs?" he teased.

She choked for a second. "Trust me, that would be a bad idea. In fact, for a wedding gift I'm considering swearing to Maggie to never attempt to sing in her presence again."

"That bad, huh?"

"Put it this way, I can hit notes they haven't invented yet."

He chuckled and she joined him in laughing, and suddenly the wall she'd wedged between them crumbled a little. They paced slowly, following Maggie and Erik on the final circle of the yard.

"So if you won't sing, will you dance with me?" Surely he could keep his feet under him for long enough to dance without making a fool of himself. Of them both.

The grip she had on his arm tightened slightly. "I'll consider it. Looks like there's a lot of single guys around to choose from."

Do not growl. Do not *growl.* It took all his strength to fight the instant urge to claim her in front of the whole damn pack. Like hell was she going to dance with anyone other than him. "I get first dance though, you know, wedding party and all."

"That might be...nice."

Nice? Bloody hell.

He ignored the questioning glances his big brother shot in his direction. Fine, maybe Pam didn't know about werewolves, and maybe he was in for a hell of a lot of trouble figuring out how he was going to solve this mess, but one thing he knew without a doubt.

She was going to be his. Body and soul.

TJ stepped around her, positioning her at Maggie's right hand. Pam shivered as he leaned in close and brushed his lips lightly against the skin beside her ear. He spoke barely above a whisper. "I guarantee it's going to be a whole lot more memorable than *nice.*"

Pam stood to the side, her fingers squeezing so hard around the flower arrangement Maggie had passed her she heard some of the flower stems crack. Across from her, TJ held her gaze with his and damn, the man was enough to distract a saint. She barely heard Erik and Maggie exchange vows, she was too caught up in admiring his clean-cut good looks. Getting lost in his mesmerizing dark eyes. She wanted to interrupt the ceremony to demand he stare elsewhere, but at the same time she couldn't help but be flattered.

Maybe a short fling wouldn't be such a bad idea after all.

The whole service passed in a blur as they locked eyes. Inside, a flame burned, desire wrapped around her core and made her heart pound. There had to be something in the northern air causing her to react like a sex-crazed ninny.

A discreet cough brought her back to her senses, and she hurried to join Maggie and Erik as they moved down the aisle between the chairs, headed for the hall. TJ's warm hand slid around her waist and goose bumps rose. He ignored her wiggled attempt to dislodge him, instead tucking her tightly against his side and lowering his head until his lips hovered an inch over her ear. She waited for him to whisper something wicked, something in keeping with the heat of passion he'd been throwing at her for the past umpteen minutes.

The anticipation was killing her and she swore her panties were wet just thinking about him saying something sexy.

"Chicken?"

Not sexy. "What?"

"Or fish? What do you want for dinner?"

She laughed out loud and relaxed against him. "You're a

goof."

TJ sighed mightily. "So I've been told."

For the next hour he proceeded to enchant her, anticipating her every need. They sat to one side of the bridal couple and throughout the meal he touched her constantly.

"You treat all your visitors like this?" she asked. Blood pounded through her hard enough she could have just finished a marathon.

TJ topped up the wine in her glass as he shook his head.

"I can honestly say you're the first woman I've ever treated this way." He rested his arm on the back of her chair and her nipples tightened. Would anyone notice if she crawled into his lap and sucked face with him for a while?

Someone at the end of the hall tinkled their wine glass, and the entire room joined in. Maggie and Erik rose good-naturedly and when he dipped her, kissing her passionately, the crowd shouted their approval. The whole event was exactly the kind of celebration Pam had hoped for her best friend.

TJ squeezed her shoulder as he stood and made his way to the front. He grabbed an acoustic guitar from somewhere and plopped himself on a stool.

A murmur rose from the crowd and TJ grinned sheepishly.

"Yeah, it's a new guitar, but this time it's not my fault. A certain little boy I was babysitting thought the old one would make a dandy boat."

Gentle laughter carried through the air as TJ tuned the strings, his fingers moving smoothly. He turned to address Erik and Maggie. "I know you requested your favourites, but if you'd humour me, I have a song I wrote a while back. I've been saving it for a special moment and I think this is about as special as it can get. It's called 'Eternal Love'."

He strummed a few chords before slipping into a simple melody, fingers picking individual notes to accompany his rich tenor. Their gazes met and he sang to her. Pam's throat tightened. She shifted uncomfortably in her chair as she listened to the lyrics. It was all so airy-fairy and impossible and yet—something deep inside wished it was possible for a love like he sang about to be real.

A love that lasted forever? Fresh each morning?

Bullshit.

Pretty sad thoughts to be entertaining while at a wedding.

She dragged her gaze off TJ to where Maggie and Erik sat staring into each other's eyes. For what it was worth, she wished them the best. Maggie deserved to be happy, and hopefully Erik was the guy to make it happen. Well, he'd damn well better or she'd rip him a new one for hurting her best friend.

Pam sighed and leaned back in her chair. She closed her eyes and let the music swirl around her. TJ's mellow voice touched her places she didn't want to think about. Places she'd closed the door on, and she'd never been one to linger over the past.

Nope, get over it and go on—that was her motto. Life was for living to the max, enjoying every experience as much as possible. One day at a time. She sat straighter and resolutely faced the singer who made her belly quiver with each new note he sang. TJ's fingers caressed the strings and she pictured him touching her with that same intensity, same attention to detail, and the pulse between her legs kicked into high gear again.

Holy Toledo, she was getting turned on watching the guy play his guitar.

What the heck had she been drinking? There was something going on, the way her gaze kept being drawn back to

TJ, the way his voice tickled in her ears and made her skin burn. The urge to go for a little tumble while she was here increased. Maggie wouldn't mind.

Besides, it wasn't like she was leaving in the morning. She had her adventure trip scheduled to start in a couple days. A few nights' excitement could be what she needed to make this a very memorable holiday.

He sang the final notes and let the tune fade away. The rest of the guests clapped and whistled in appreciation. TJ finally broke eye contact with her and smiled out at the crowd, before motioning for a few others to join him. They picked up instruments and the group hit into a lively tune. Chairs and tables were dragged aside, and the hall became a bustling hive of noise as everyone stepped in to rearrange and make space for dancing. Pam moved a couple chairs before realizing she was more of a hindrance than help. She snuck to the side and watched in fascination as the room transformed before her eyes. Up on the stage TJ and another guitarist strummed something with a hard-rock beat, and the rhythm pulsed in time with her heart. His dark hair shone in the light as he rocked, and she wondered if it would feel fine or coarse if she ran her fingers through it.

"Did you enjoy that?" Maggie asked.

Pam jumped a little, then let out the breath she'd been holding. "Hey. Fabulous ceremony, and the meal was delicious."

Her friend nodded in agreement. "It was good, but I meant the singing. I didn't expect TJ to share a song he'd written himself. It was beautiful."

"He's got a great voice," Pam admitted. Maggie smiled past her and Pam glanced over her shoulder to see Erik hanging back. "You guys taking off soon?"

Her friend nodded. "I wanted to make sure everything was

kosher with you. We'll be back tomorrow afternoon, and have some more time to visit before you take off on your excursion and we leave on our honeymoon." She wrinkled her nose. "You going to be okay with us leaving you? Because I could—"

Pam slapped a hand over her friend's mouth for a second. "Oh no, girlfriend. You weren't about to suggest you'd stick around on your wedding night to babysit me, were you?"

"Hell, no." Maggie grinned. "I was going to say if you wanted to you could go home early and hide. I've got all your favourite videos and there's microwave popcorn in the cupboard."

Pam deliberately glanced around, eyeing the smartly dressed men before turning to smirk at Maggie. "You think I want to go watch *Serenity* for the millionth time when you've got this kind of a smorgasbord laid out for me?"

"They are kind of tasty, aren't they?" Maggie turned and they both gazed out into the room.

It was a little annoying that the first place her gaze went was to where TJ stood. *Shoot.* Pam ignored the blatant interest running on a constant loop in her brain and grinned evilly. "Oh yeah, and there's one in particular who's been making me drool all afternoon."

"Really?" Maggie leaned closer and whispered. "Who?"

"That one." Pam pointed at Erik and laughed out loud when Maggie elbowed her.

"Hands off, sugar, get your own Friendly Giant."

The music started again, a slow tempo this time and Maggie pulled Pam in for a hug. "Time for the first dance, then Erik and I are going to sneak away. I'll see you at dinner tomorrow, okay?"

Pam kissed her cheek quickly. "Don't worry about me. It's not like you're throwing me to the dogs."

Maggie snorted loudly. "At least you know how to handle them."

"Trust me, I can handle the two-legged variety as well as I deal with the four-legged. Now go on, your big brute is waiting and even though I still think I could take him down, I'm going to be nice and not hurt him before you get to enjoy tonight."

Erik held out his hand and Maggie joined him with a laugh and the two of them spun off onto the dance floor. Pam let out a long, slow breath. It was clear they were very much in love. Maybe it would work out. The lights of the hall dimmed and a disco ball turned on. Pam fought back a snicker as sparkles danced over the walls and the lone pair in the spotlight.

Someone stepped in behind her, the heat of his solid body hitting her back as he wrapped his hands around her waist and gently nestled them together.

TJ.

Cocky bastard, really. She debated slamming a heel on his instep, or flipping him over her shoulder, just to teach him a lesson, but watching Maggie and Erik float around the floor had mellowed her too much.

"You should be careful putting the moves on a girl like that. You might lose something important," she warned.

He ignored the threat and rested his chin on her shoulder. The heat radiating between them tempted her. "They fit awesome together, don't they?"

His breath brushed her cheek, warm and sweet smelling. Her mouth watered, but she didn't want to talk romance with him.

"They look...unbalanced. What was Maggie thinking getting involved with someone so much taller than her?"

He *hmmed*. "They were probably thinking that when it's

right, there's no denying you've found the one you want."

Oh lordy, his thumbs stroked her waist, and he nuzzled under her ear. Did she want this? Heat flushed her. She had to decide, and quick. She could lead him out onto the dance floor and enjoy his touch in public, or they could find a dark corner and see what else came up.

So to speak.

He tugged her backward and her body overruled her mind. They slipped into the shadows at the side of the hall, ducking behind a room divider. He pressed her against it, his solid body very, very warm. Her heart rate increased, as did the tingling sensation between her thighs, and she squeezed her legs together to stop the ache.

Man-oh-man, his eyes were so incredible she swore he was using some kind of hypnosis. Turning away was impossible as he stared at her, tracing her hair, her face, one finger outlining her lips before he slowly lowered his head and brought their mouths together.

He brushed his lips over hers like a gentle breeze, his fingers tugging her hair to redirect the angle of her head until their mouths meshed together. Tentative strokes of his tongue brushed fleetingly past her teeth. Teasing, barely giving her a taste of him before he broke away and dropped his forehead against hers.

"Holy shit, you taste good," he panted. "Incredibly fabulous. I'd never dreamed a woman could taste like you. Or make me feel the way you make me feel."

Screw the sweet talk. She hadn't had nearly enough of his kisses. She tried to regain possession of his lips. Arched her back in an attempt to press their bodies together and let her feel his muscles, his desire for her.

He groaned softly. "You're killing me. We shouldn't..."

150

She stepped on either side of his leg and pasted her aching crotch to his thigh. A short gasp escaped her as the impact made her clit throb.

"Fuck it." TJ grabbed her butt and dragged her hard against him, wrestling control from her as this time he kissed her senseless. Sucked the air from her lungs, twined their tongues together. An almost desperate, mindless, seeking touch. He demanded her response and she gave it eagerly. The pleasure in her sex rose like a rocket blasting into outer space.

His hands were everywhere. Skimming her torso, touching her breasts. Clutching her hips and grinding her hard onto his thigh. Excitement washed over her, the rapid beat of her pulse making her lightheaded, out of breath. He licked a path down her neck, nibbled on her collarbone and something electric shot to her core.

"I want you, Pam," he growled against her skin. "You're going to be mine."

Sheesh, that comment pushed a few wrong buttons, but right here, right now? She wasn't about to argue with his macho-sexist statement as long as he kept doing what he was doing. Lost beyond all reason, she teetered on the edge of an orgasm and if he stopped she would kill him. Pam clasped his head in her hands and hauled his mouth to hers as she leaned back and tried to find the final touch she needed to go over the edge.

The barrier at her back wobbled for a second, then tilted to the north. All their weight went with the wall as it tipped, crashing to the floor with them on top. She smothered her curses as the flames of desire building between them evaporated into thin air.

TJ's heavy breathing echoed in her ear as they unwound tangled limbs. The damn disco lights flickered over them, showcasing their undignified situation. Partygoers congregated to stare with concern and offer helping hands. Pam scrambled to her feet, but all she could think about was the aching need in her core and the sweet taste of him lingering in her mouth.

Chapter Three

Keil pinched the bridge of his nose and TJ attempted to stand in one place and not fidget like a naughty school kid hauled in front of the principal.

"She's your mate."

"Screw it, Keil, I've told you a dozen times. If all you're going to do is repeat 'she's your mate' in a tone of voice suggesting I'm more than slightly brain-dead, we're hardly going to get anywhere with this conversation, are we?"

Robyn laughed.

"It's not funny," Keil complained.

Robyn tugged his arm and cupped her mate's face in her hands, staring into his eyes.

TJ watched as his brother and sister-in-law discussed him. He knew they were doing it, that talking-between-themselves thing mates could do. He sighed. Well, most mates. He doubted he and Pam would be able to, since she wasn't wolf. Still, he wasn't going to argue with fate.

She was most definitely the one. Kissing the woman had been better than any sexual experience he'd had before in his life. He'd been rapidly approaching the point where he would have embarrassed himself and come in his pants. Then he'd managed, again, to muck things up.

So now he waited to be disciplined like a disobedient puppy by his Alpha pair. What he wanted to do was figure out a way to find Pam and finish what they'd started. If she'd even speak to him after being rescued from the tangled mess they'd ended up in on the floor. Thankfully the lights had been dim enough everyone thought it was nothing more than his usual clumsy self, and not the two of them fooling around, that caused the accident.

A tug on his sleeve brought him back from his mental wanderings. Robyn smiled at him and used American Sign Language to talk to him. She signed slowly—he had learned a lot, but still wasn't fluent.

"If Pam is your mate, how are you going to deal with it?"

TJ hesitated. "You mean, like will I tell her about being a wolf?"

Robyn nodded.

Shit, he hadn't thought about that. Hell if he knew. He tapped his right fingertips against his forehead several times then flung his hand to the right, ending with his palm out and all five fingers raised.

Robyn blew out a long, slow breath. "You don't know. So if we suggest you proceed slowly until you have figured it out, would that make sense?"

Fuck. "Why do you have to be so logical?" he complained.

"Would you prefer we ordered you to stay away from her until she leaves Alaska?" his brother asked. Keil came and stood next to Robyn, the two of them together an immovable wall.

"She's my mate. You wouldn't be so cruel." *Would they?*

"We're not trying to hurt you, but we have to figure out the best thing for the entire pack. If she is your mate, and I'm not denying it, it's going to make things bloody awkward around here." Keil crossed his arms and leaned back on the table. "We've finally got the pack to the point they aren't complaining about full-blood and half-breed issues nearly so much, and now this?"

TJ ran a hand through his hair in frustration. "I didn't do it on purpose."

"No, but it's potentially pretty volatile to have a full human enter the mix."

"I'm not giving her up."

Robyn shook her head. She pushed Keil until he moved his bulk away with a sigh. "Fine, you talk to him. I'm going back to the party to make sure none of the pack gets into too much shit."

Keil kissed Robyn before he left—a sweet and tender kiss—and TJ's throat tightened with something between happiness and envy. He'd always wanted to have a mate. To have someone to care for and enjoy their company, like he'd witnessed between his older brother and his wife. And now? It was potentially within his grasp.

Robyn settled on the couch. She checked him over carefully and TJ's skin crawled.

"If you're planning on using your Super Alpha Powers of Obedience on me, I want to say upfront—that would totally suck."

She laughed as she lifted her hands to sign at him. "Keil tries so hard to be fair to the pack he forgets to be fair to you. No alpha shit, just one question."

He sat across from her. In the past two and a half years since Robyn had joined the pack, she'd come a long way from being clueless about werewolves. Being deaf didn't stop her from being one of the most powerful—and creative—leaders he'd ever known. Maybe she had an idea of how he should deal with the mess.

"One question?"

"You don't know if she wants you…"

Well, if the little episode in the hall meant anything.

"…for anything other than a fling." Robyn stared expectantly.

Damn. "She's my—"

"Mate. I know, but she's not a wolf. You want her, and will always want her, but I don't think it works the same with humans, does it?"

TJ shrugged. "Never thought about it. I mean, I know there are wolves and humans who are married, but most of them are outcast wolves, who live packless…"

His stomach fell. If he took Pam as a mate, would they expect him to leave? Granite Lake had always been his home, and while his mate was of vital importance, he didn't want to give up his pack. His family. He dropped his head into his hands. Suddenly what should have been the most fabulous day of his life turned grey and cold.

Robyn touched his shoulder gently to get his attention. "We will never kick you out. If Pam is your mate, she's a part of our family, no matter what."

She stared at him for a little while and a nervous twitch started in his thigh. He jiggled his legs to try and hide his reaction. This was a lot more complicated than he'd ever expected it to be. Inside, his wolf fidgeted. It couldn't understand why they were sitting here instead of sniffing out the delicious-smelling female who belonged to them.

"You need to give her time. If she accepts you as a human, you'll have a better chance of her accepting you as a wolf. You can't go off half-cocked on this one, TJ. Take the time, do it right and make it last."

TJ snorted in derision. "How?"

"She's registered for the next expedition with Keil's wilderness excursion company. You're going along as a guide. Give her a chance to get to know you a little better in a setting you're comfortable in. See what happens, more than just physical attraction. But you must control your wolf."

He and Keil had already been preparing for the next wilderness trip. There was a group of ten signed up, including Pam. While he appreciated Robyn had a point, having to court his mate around a large group of people was stupid. There might be safety in numbers and everything, but he didn't want to have numbers. One plus one would be fine, thank you very much. An idea rumbled in the back of his mind and he tried very hard not to let anything show on his face. An excursion? Some time alone?

Oh yeah.

Loud clapping shook him from his reverie. Robyn lowered her hands and glared at him.

He leapt to his feet. "Sure, sounds great. Awesome idea, you know, taking some time to get to know her. You're a genius. Gorgeous, and a genius. What did Keil ever do without you?" *Babbling.* He was officially babbling.

How fast could he get out of the room before she figured out something was amiss? He flashed her two thumbs up and dodged a footrest, aiming for the front door. "Well, gotta run. Lots to do in the next couple of days. Gotta get lots of sleep and keep my head and stay in control, right?"

He ducked outside before she could say anything like "What the hell are you planning and I forbid you to even think about pulling a fast one." 'Cause what he had in mind was definitely on the not-going-to-be-approved list.

But this was his *mate* they were talking about here. Like Keil had waited longer than a day to claim Robyn. TJ headed back toward the hall, a brisk five-minute walk up the gravel road from his Alpha's house. The music of the party carried through the air, and he hurried as fast as possible. The thought of finding Pam dancing with any of the other guys made the hair at the back of his neck stand upright. Oh no, waiting was out of the question. He pulled out his cell phone and made the first call. "Hey, Jared? Get your ass off the dance floor for five minutes. I need to talk to you."

Pam threw herself on the couch in Maggie's living room and groaned in frustration. Off in the distance she still heard dance music, but she'd lost interest after getting tossed to the ground like a piece of confetti. Well, not true. She'd brushed herself off, thankful for the dim lighting so no one saw how flushed her cheeks were. Still, accidents happen, and she'd been more than happy to head out onto the dance floor when the man of the moment had disappeared.

Great. So much for forever, the guy couldn't even stick around for long enough to finish giving her an orgasm.

She clicked on the TV and flicked through channels listlessly. Maggie was gone with her true love, sexing it up wherever their bridal suite was. Pam had the run of the house and all she could think about was how lonely it was going to be to crawl into bed tonight.

Gack. Horny and morose, what an insipid combination. She was well on the way to hitting all the high notes for a pity party in under an hour.

The door to the kitchen creaked, moving an inch, and she sat up to stare at it. She hadn't heard anyone come in, but what with all the fun she was having watching *The Price is Right*, there could have been a dozen people in the next room.

"Hello?"

The door shifted again, and this time a silver-grey muzzle appeared, poking through the crack. Pam frowned. She didn't know Maggie and Erik had a dog. She knelt on the seat cushion and watched more carefully. The animal took a few cautious sniffs, its nostrils flaring.

"Hey, what you doing?" All the signs were there for her to read—classic nonaggressive behavior, curiosity more than anything. Pam smiled. "Come on, don't be afraid."

Even though the beast didn't act hostile, once its full head popped through the doorway, Pam swore.

"Holy shit, no one told me they kept wolves as pets here. Good...wolfie. Stay."

The silver-grey creature had made it into the room and obediently sat at her command. Pam blew out a slow breath of air. Thank God for well-trained animals. She came around the couch cautiously to examine the wolf. It seemed to be staring back just as intently, panting softly, its tongue lolling to one side. She held out a hand and allowed herself to be sniffed.

"So, I've got a buddy for tonight. You tired of dancing as well? Going to hang with me for a girl's night out?"

The wolf snorted, a gust of air rushing past her hand. Pam touched the animal's muzzle gently, brushing the coarse fur, rubbing its ears.

"There you go. It's okay. I'm not going to hurt you." What a beautiful creature. She wasn't sure what other lineage had been crossbred with the wolf, but the mix was stunning. Its fur was soft—softer than the German Shepherds she was used to working with. Pam unconsciously examined the beast like she would any of her partners. Whoever owned this animal took excellent care of it. She passed a hand along its belly and laughed when he jerked back.

"Oops, not a girl. Sorry about that. Still, I'd be glad for you to stick around if you don't have any big plans for the night."

She rose and the wolf stepped beside her heels. Very well trained, and to be honest, just the kind of company she needed after the strange ending to her evening. Pam curled up in the corner of the couch. The wolf laid its chin on her knee and stared at her with a completely lovelorn expression. She rubbed his head again. She loved how completely honest and simple an animal's affection was. You could trust them to act according to normal patterns.

She missed her partner, but it had been time to let him retire.

"You like comedy or action movies better, wolfie? Come on, hop up. Maybe you're not allowed on the couch usually, but tonight is a special deal." She patted the seat beside her and suddenly there was a large furry rug draping itself over her legs. She scratched his neck, checking for a collar and a dog tag. "I don't understand why the heck people don't collar their pets. What am I going to call you?"

A long wet tongue smeared its way up the side of her cheek and she laughed out loud.

"Cool it, I don't need a bath." She grabbed him by the scruff of the neck and maneuvered him into a less accessible position. It might be a way of showing affection, but canine slobber wasn't her favourite. She clicked the TV back on and tried to get into the show.

It was impossible. The edginess that had started earlier in the day still rode her hard. Damn TJ for getting her motor running then abandoning her. She tangled her fingers in the wolf's fur and tried to relax. The lingering heat of the day and the rest of the day's excitement finally got to her. Plus the warmth radiating from the wolf as he lay nestled alongside her. There was something comforting about having an animal around. She missed her partner. When she caught herself yawning for the third time in rapid succession she gave up, clicked off the screen and stretched lazily.

"Okay, wolfie. Time for you to head home." She rose to push open the kitchen door only to see the animal's rump disappear up the stairs. "Hey, where do you think you're going?"

When she found him curled up on her bed, she laughed. "Bet you're a bed hog. Fine, as long as you don't snore, you can stay."

She stripped off the sweats she'd changed into after abandoning the party before pulling on an oversized T-shirt. One hard shove moved him over enough she could crawl under the quilt. He didn't do any of the usual canine things to settle down, just stuck his nose by her ear and licked her once before plopping on his belly close to her side. She chuckled and draped an arm over him.

Sometime during the night when she rolled over, he was gone. How poetic, she'd been dumped by another male. She sighed and slipped back into her dreams.

Chapter Four

Glorious blue sky greeted them for the first day of the tour. With the weather cooperating, Pam checked out the other hikers with a wary eye. This was the biggest concern she'd had with Maggie's suggestion she take part in an organized expedition—you never knew who your companions would be, and at times too many people made for trouble.

Keil called for everyone's attention before pointing at the stack of supplies piled on the picnic table.

"We've got light daypacks for everyone, already loaded with snacks and water bottles. Don't try to race up the hill, take your time and enjoy the journey. There are a number of set places we'll stop and have photo ops, but anytime you need to stop and take a stretch break, feel free. We've got enough guides you can all go at your own pace."

Pam nodded in satisfaction. It appeared there were a few different fitness levels within the group, and while she wasn't sure how fast she'd be hiking, it was nice to know Keil didn't expect them to stick in one mass pack. She stared up at King's Throne peak towering over her and adjusted the light pack to sit a little easier. Clear sky, soft fragrant breeze—should be an awesome day ahead. She turned and bumped into TJ.

"Hey there, ready for the hike?"

She pretended to be annoyed. "Are you planning on dogging

my heels the entire week I'm with the excursion?"

He wrinkled his nose. "Umm, pretty much the plan, yeah. Or at least until you accept my apology. I didn't mean to desert you the other night."

Pam laughed softly. The guy was nothing if not persistent. "I know, you were called away momentarily and when you got back I was gone. It's okay, I forgive you. Really."

"Why are you acting like you'd enjoy seeing me...fall in the lake or something?"

Tempting thought. Only because she bet he'd look great dripping wet, his clothes clinging to him. Maybe she could convince him it would be better to let them air dry and he would hike in the nude.

Yeah, right, with nine other people around?

He gestured down the path and she fell into step with him. "I was upset, but I'm done. It just wasn't how I expected to spend the evening."

She heard his quick intake of air. Yeah, his response was pretty much her response.

She'd given it a lot of thought over the past two days as she got ready for the trip—especially after finding out TJ was one of the guides. She could stay mad and pout, or turn it around and have some fun. Since this was her chance to get out and have a good time, she chose to give him a break. There was too much attraction between them to be upset for any length of time, and really, wasn't it a waste of energy? She'd be gone in a couple of weeks and in the meantime he could show her some Northern Hospitality.

But making him squirm was still fun.

They walked easily along the wide section of trail. "Is this an old road?"

"Logging road. The trail narrows when we reach the Cottonwood Junction. Then it's single file until we reach the meadow."

They chatted about the Yukon Territory. TJ pointed out some of the more unusual plants at their feet. "The wildflowers are pretty much all gone by now, except the fireweed."

"It's pretty."

"It's a weed, but yes, a pretty one."

Hours passed, and she fell into a rhythm, gazing out over the scenery and enjoying the chance for a physical challenge. A couple of the hikers in the group had fallen a fair ways behind, and soon there were only two others in the group with her and TJ.

"How long are you spending in the Yukon?" one of the men asked. She slid a little farther away from him. While he wouldn't be a physical challenge to her, she didn't feel like flirting with anyone. Anyone other than TJ, that is.

"Couple of weeks, right?" TJ stepped between them before gesturing to the right and directing their attention to a lookout point.

Pam hid her smile.

The panoramic views when they reached the top were staggeringly beautiful. Pam wandered aimlessly and clicked picture after picture. Tufts of clouds clinging to the mountaintops. A ribbon of glacier ice trailing off into the distance. The sun reflecting in a million dazzling light spots on the surface of Kathleen Lake.

Every time she glanced up she found TJ's gaze fixed on her.

"Don't you have anyone else you need to take care of?"

He shook his head slowly. "I set up the picnic already, and everyone else is eating. I had to make sure you didn't stroll too close to the edge of the mountain or anything."

Oh dear, it was hot up here, under the blazing heat of his stare.

"If there's a picnic, I guess I should go join them."

"I kept some out for us. We can eat here. Alone."

Pam concentrated hard. *Okey dokey.*

They sat together, TJ pointing in various directions and naming the local mountaintops visible from their vantage point. Pam nibbled on her sandwich, all the while trying to think of a good excuse to bring up the aborted kiss from the other night. As in, maybe they should find a way and means to try it again.

She'd never been so attracted to a man and so tongue-tied. There didn't seem to be any appropriate openings, and she wasn't about to simply jump him.

Well, not yet.

"So, I was thinking." TJ passed her a juice box, condensation beading its surface.

"Dangerous thing to do."

He grinned. "I'd like to make it up to you, I mean, leaving you in the lurch the other day. I kinda hoped you would forgive me enough to accept a little peace offering."

Hmmm, bribery totally worked. "Like extra chocolate bars? Dark? I'd be willing to forgive just about anything for chocolate."

His laugh rolled over her as he grabbed his daypack.

"That's not the surprise, but I think I can still help you out." He dug out a Ziploc bag and reached in for an extra-large foil-wrapped bar. "Oops, it's too warm today to be hauling chocolate. Sorry."

He pulled one out. Chocolate oozed from the edges and ran down his fingers. *Hello opportunity.* She grabbed his hand.

"No problem, I like it this way."

She brought his hand to her mouth and sucked one digit in, licking the warm melted gooeyness clean before moving to the next one. His breathing sped up and her pussy grew wet. Okay, she was over being mad and there had better be private rooms available wherever they were staying tonight.

By the time she removed all traces of chocolate, she could barely breathe. He leaned toward her, his dark eyes fixing her in place as their lips touched.

Bells rang. Cool, they weren't even kissing and she heard bells.

TJ pulled away with a sigh and her hopes faded. It was a real bell and it was moving closer. "There's the signal to round everyone up and start the journey down the hill." He stared at her lips. "Remember where we were…"

Oh boy.

Pam gathered her wits as best she could and scrambled to her feet. He aimed her in the right direction, and she shook her head as she hit the trail. Okay, he was fine enough looking, but she must have some kind of altitude fever. She watched him out of the corner of her eye until he caught her.

Focus on the trail. There will be plenty of time to flirt later if I don't trip and break my neck.

Half an hour later he caught up with her, tugging gently on her hand to get her attention.

"You interested in a little aerial sightseeing? My treat."

"You serious? When?"

TJ grinned and pulled her against him, hiding her from the others as they disappeared around the corner. He leaned closer and whispered in her ear. "In about an hour. I've arranged for a chopper to pick us up back in the meadow where we stopped for our first snack break this morning."

His warm breath caressed her neck and a shiver raced over her skin. Holy hell, the man made her horny without even trying.

"So is this like a private event or are we taking any of the others along as well?" She tilted her head to indicate the guy who had tried to hit on her earlier.

"Very private. There's room for you and me and the pilot. So, you have to do a couple things. Number one." He kissed her neck and slipped his hand into her hair to nestle her a little closer.

"Number one?" Lordy, was that her voice? That throaty, sexy, fuck-me-in-the-meadow voice?

"Hmm, you can't tell anyone we're going." He nibbled on her earlobe and she moaned. *Oh yeah.*

"I can do that. I'm real good at keeping secrets."

"I bet you are. The second thing..." He stroked a hand down her back until he cupped her butt and she was ready to crawl up his body.

"Second...thing. Damn it, TJ, you keep touching me and I won't remember a word you've said."

"All you need to remember is when the chopper lands, crouch low and come to the door quickly. We want to get away without upsetting the other customers too much, okay?"

"Are you going to get in trouble for this?"

He didn't answer, just tugged her closer and took her lips. Hokie spit, the guy could kiss. His lips alone started reactions that other lovers had to work up to with a full dinner, dance and a couple of bottles of wine. When he finally broke off, she had to gasp for air. He smiled at her, his thumb brushing her cheek gently.

"Some troubles are completely worth the risk."

He drew apart and held a finger to his lips. She nodded. It would be nice to be able to get away from the group. She'd flown in choppers, but only for work. Excitement made her shiver.

"Where are we going to go?"

"Fly over a bit of the Kluane National Park. You'll be able to see Mount Logan before we'll head over the glacier field and past a couple of beautiful lakes."

She grabbed his hand and squeezed it. "Thanks, TJ. This is very considerate. I'm looking forward to spending a little time alone with you." His eyes flashed dark and he gazed the length of her body before dragging himself away.

"Remember that. Time alone is a good thing."

TJ listened intently for the sound of the chopper. It was going to all come down to timing. The pilot was a friend of his, and hopefully Shaun had managed to get everything in place.

Now to make sure Keil didn't interrupt his plans.

The group had spread out like they usually did by this time during a hike. The more eager people had stayed high to do a little extra exploring. Keil had begun the downward journey with the slower-moving crew to give them extra time to make it to the parking lot and the picnic supper being prepared for them.

Pam took a swallow from her water bottle and licked her lips, and his cock jerked to life again. He'd been pretty much hard since two nights ago when she'd stripped in front of him. The memory of her naked torso before she'd pulled on a sleep shirt—the image was as clear as a picture and it haunted him.

His mate was exactly what he desired in a woman. He'd had to leave before he was too tempted to shift out of his wolf and crawl all over her. No, this was far better. Time alone. That was the goal, wasn't it? He heard the faint sound of Shaun's chopper in the distance grow nearer.

"Come on, let's head to the edge of the meadow."

She took his hand and he had to ignore the electric shock that flew through him. He wondered if his touch had the same effect on her as on him. There was no doubt in his mind they would be fabulous together. Not just sex, although, hello, that was looking to be spectacular as well, but she seemed so understanding and he was looking forward to the next week. Finding out what it meant to have someone to lavish all his attention on. All his love.

He needed to pull off one last maneuver.

The volume and wind movement increased as the helicopter hovered overhead and Pam hid her face against his chest. His arm around her shoulders felt so good and natural he knew there must be a big goofy grin on his face. He protected her until the runners settled and the door swung open.

His friend Jared jumped out, flashed a thumbs-up and sprinted to the edge of the field. TJ guided Pam and popped her into the cabin, climbed after her and shut the door firmly. She searched for seatbelts and he reached to help her, then tapped Shaun on the shoulder. When the clamor of the props increased to painful decibels, he grabbed the headsets hanging on the sidewall. After slipping hers on, he showed her the buttons to press to talk.

"You comfy?" He rearranged the daypacks at their feet, leaning closer under the disguise of adjusting her seatbelt.

"Great. Where are we headed?"

Paradise, he hoped. "Look out the left window, there's

Mount Logan. Almost twenty thousand feet or six thousand metres, it's the tallest in Canada and second tallest in North America."

She leaned across his body to see out his side window and her hair fell like a curtain across him. Sweet smelling. A combination of jasmine and her own natural scent. The one that made his eyes cross and his pants grow far too tight.

"Gorgeous. Is that the glacier you mentioned?"

He pointed out the other window, wrapped his arm around her and carried on with the tour. Every trip he'd done over the past years came in handy as he managed to answer most of her questions.

The tour also helped time to pass. Once out of Kluane National Park, they dipped around Sheep Mountain, leaving behind the Alaskan highway to head deeper into the bush. Thick forest spread under them, rising and falling in endless green waves. Shaun gestured in the air and TJ's excitement rose. They were almost there. He squeezed Pam's fingers. Somehow her hand had found its way into his and he didn't want to let go.

"You want to land?" he asked her.

She grinned at him. "You mean it?"

Outside the window was the foot of a pristine mountain lake, a field of wild grasses stretching from the shore toward the tree-covered foothills of the mountain. Shaun maneuvered his way to the north where a sparkling brook raced into the lake. He settled the chopper in a small meadow, and TJ cracked open the door, hopped out and reached to help Pam.

Of course, when she lost her balance and landed on top of him he was torn between cursing his bad luck and longing to stay there forever.

Stick to the plan. "It's noisy here. Let's move a bit."

170

"Is he going to stop the propellers?"

Highly unlikely, but he wasn't going to tell her that. Yet. She laughed as he rolled, bringing her to her feet and running away from the chopper until they could speak without shouting.

"Do we have long enough I can go touch the lake?"

"Sure." He followed her, and she spun her arms out in a circle, breathing in huge drafts of the air. She looked wild and alive and vital, and he was head over heels in love.

"Race you." She was off. TJ chased her, catching her before they lost the grass underfoot. He tackled her carefully, twisting as they fell to put her in his arms, resting on top of him. It took a second for the utter shock of having succeeded without breaking bones, his or hers, to fully register.

"Well, hello. Weren't we here a couple of minutes ago?" Pam teased, resting her elbows on his chest and cradling her chin in her hands.

"I think we were almost here. There's one thing missing."

He cupped her head and lowered her lips to his. Her taste twined around him and sucked him under, the feel of his mate resting on top of him the best thing he'd ever experienced.

She responded with enthusiasm, exploring with her tongue, kissing him back with as much passion as he wished. She pulled her legs up to straddle him and her warm crotch rested on his groin. A faint movement of her hips and the contact increased. Oh hell, he was going to explode if she wiggled again.

Pam sat upright, the highlights in her hair shining red in the sun's bright light. She grinned at him. "Well, I seem to have you at my mercy, but we probably need to be going soon, right?"

The loudening *flap flap* of the propeller blades reached them, and her eyes widened. "What's he doing?"

She scrambled to the side, and her jaw fell open as the chopper lifted. The air pressure flattened them to the ground as Shaun got away. TJ waved at his friend as the aircraft rose, hovering over the field for a moment before rotating and taking off into the distance.

"What is going on? Stop it...come back." Pam ran after the helicopter, waving her arms frantically before returning, her beautiful brown eyes wide. "He left us. What is he doing?"

TJ stood and pulled her back into his arms. "Don't worry, it's okay. He'll be back."

She relaxed. "Well, that's good. How long do we have before he returns?"

"A week."

Chapter Five

Pam stared at him. What kind of...? It had to be a joke.

"No, seriously. Does he need to get fuel or something?"

"Nope, he's got a few other things to do, but he'll be back for us. Eventually. You want to help me carry our packs to the cabin?" TJ turned to step toward the center of the meadow.

Cabin? She grabbed him by the arm and whipped him back to face her. "You're shitting me, aren't you? You really just had us dumped in the bush? Are you insane?"

"Look, it's going to be fine. Let's grab our stuff and we can talk about it more once we're settled."

She bit her tongue. Seriously, the guy must not be firing on all rockets, but humouring him for a moment was the only solution. She stared around the meadow a little more intently. "Where is everything? The cabin, the food, the bathhouse with the running water and satellite TV?"

"No TV, but I do promise running water. Come on."

He led her to the spot the helicopter had landed. There, where the grass lay low from the air from the propellers compressing it flat, sat a box and two full-sized backpacks. One of them was her own bright red pack she could have sworn she'd left safely back at the expedition van.

He shouldered his pack and the box, grinned at her and led

her toward the trees.

Okay. She was going to kill him, but after she had a roof over her head. She shrugged on her pack and followed behind.

The trail led to a neat log cabin facing the lake. It was tucked in so tight she hadn't even noticed it earlier, but now she appreciated the setting. Once she got past the part of her that wanted to take TJ apart, this wasn't a bad place.

He stopped at the bottom of the wide staircase leading up to the sturdy wood door.

"A private getaway just for you. I know I should have checked with you first, but I needed to make things happen pretty quick. I figured asking for forgiveness would be easier than asking permission."

She stared at him in disbelief. This wasn't happening. Her heart pounded, blood rushing past her temples so hard her vision blurred. She wasn't sure if it was from shock or because she was pissed off.

Pissed off. Definitely the one to go with. The man needed to be handled, and she had the touch. Pam calmed her expression and spoke softly.

"So what you're trying to tell me is you deliberately set this up. The remote cabin, the whole 'just us by ourselves' thing?"

He nodded, a twinkle in his eye.

"Ahhh, that's so..." She stepped closer and patted him on the cheek. "How incredibly..."

With one quick movement she grabbed his ear and twisted, hard. He clutched her hand and dropped to his knees. "Shit, wait."

She glared daggers at him. "I can't believe you're such a schmuck. Who in the hell put you in charge of me? Did you ask? Did you even consider maybe what I signed up for was what I wanted to take part in? Idiot." An extra twist accompanied her final word and TJ yowled through clenched teeth.

"Arghhh, I have the list of all the things you wanted to try. We'll make it happen here, only a little more enjoyable because there won't be crowds around."

She let go of his ear and stomped across the porch. *Unbelievable.* "You kidnapped me."

"Wait, it's not like that." He scrambled to his feet, patting all his pockets frantically. "Ah, fuck, I'm screwing this all up. I didn't say it right. I meant to... I wanted to *ask* you if you would like to stay here. We can still call the helicopter back. Just..."

TJ tossed the pack off his back and flipped open zippers, obviously looking for something. Pam lowered her pack as well, dropping it against the side of the cabin. She wanted her hands and feet clear if she needed to kick his butt. She assumed a defensive crouch, ready to smack him to the ground if necessary.

He twirled toward her. Something dark thrust her direction and she moved instinctively, the side of her hand cracking his forearm hard enough to bruise. As he cried out, an oblong shape flew from his fingers and slammed into the door. Pieces of black plastic rained down on the porch boards, a set of batteries rolling and spinning back from the wall, finally coming to a stop against her foot.

Fuck.

Pam knelt and picked up the mangled body of the transceiver, snapped wires dangling from the case. One round dial fell to the ground and spun like a top, the echo of the *whirl whirl* fading until the piece tipped over with a soft *plop.*

TJ cleared his throat.

She pinned her lips together. Letting out a shriek of

laughter right now probably wasn't the most mature response, but...oh my God. It was a full minute before she could speak.

"That was a satellite phone?" She was proud of how calm she sounded. Not on the verge of hysteria or anything.

"Umm, right. So we could call Shaun back if you didn't want to stay."

Pam closed her eyes and counted to ten. Two wrongs didn't make a right, but it appeared his mistake coupled with hers did make them stranded.

"That was our only phone?"

"Yup."

His honest answer amused the heck out of her and suddenly most of her bluster drained away. "I'm upset with you. Don't get me wrong, I'm still planning on getting my revenge. But in a kind of twisted way, you bringing me here is sweet. Psycho, but sweet."

"Twisted and sweet. I'll take it." He gave her the most disarming puppy-dog look, and she bit her lip to stop from laughing.

He opened the door and motioned for her to enter first. She grabbed her pack, crunching a couple of pieces of plastic underfoot as she stepped inside. The cabin was bright and cheery, and bigger than she'd expected. The main area held an open sitting room with a mini kitchen on one side and a beautiful stone fireplace on the opposite wall. Two doors opened off the back, and after dropping her pack to the floor, she peeked her head into the first to find a bedroom. Damn, that wasn't a king-size either, more like a king plus.

"I have to do a couple of things outside. Look around, get settled." TJ took off quickly and she let out a big breath.

Holy crap, they were stuck here. She should be absolutely

furious. How could anyone in this day and age think it was okay to take a person somewhere without permission? Yet as she wandered the cabin, she wasn't really upset. She had wanted to have an adventure, and signing up for the expedition had been more Maggie's idea than her own.

It was partly her fault for overreacting on the stairs. Oh God. She laughed at herself, shaking her head as she wandered the cabin. This—enforced solitude—was what she truly wanted right now. Add the fact that TJ, Mr. Turns-me-on-without-even-trying, was the one she was staying with? She stared at the monstrous bed again. Okay. She was the one out of her mind, but this could actually be a lot of fun.

Of course she still planned on making him suffer. She should be able to get a few backrubs, maybe even a foot massage, out of him if he felt guilty enough.

She spotted a broom in the corner and took a few passes, but there wasn't anything underfoot that shouldn't be there. She checked the cupboards, looked under the bed...no dust, no signs of mice. The cupboards were full with dry goods and snacks. It was the cleanest cabin she'd ever seen. Cleaner than her apartment since Maggie moved out, if she was honest.

Heavy footsteps landed on the porch boards and she hurried out of the bedroom to see TJ shoulder his way into the front room, his arms around a paper bag. He watched her closely and she sighed.

"I'm not going to hit you over the head with the cast-iron frying pan I found, if that's what you're worried about."

He grinned. "Good, 'cause we'll need that for breakfast, and pancakes cook better in undented pans."

She laughed. "Okay, we'll talk about the abduction in more detail later. Can I help you put things away?"

The bottom of the paper bag he held gave way, sending the

contents to the floor in a cascading avalanche. They both scrambled to catch things but in the end most of it ended up in a heap at their feet. She bent to help gather the scented candles, chocolates, massage oil, extra-large box of condoms... Heat raced over her as she held it up, staring at his bright red face.

"Got plans?"

He swallowed a few times nervously. "Only if you do."

Oh lordy. She needed to regain a little control, and holding the evidence of what could happen very shortly was not making this any easier. She stepped back. "I think...I need some fresh air."

"Why don't you let me clean up and put stuff away? You can go..."

"I'll check out the lake..."

They spoke simultaneously. It was too much and she fled, racing out the door to where the evening breeze carried over the water.

Two more seconds and she would have had him using one of the condoms.

The trail straight in front of the cabin led her to a tiny dock extending over the water. She pulled off her shoes and dangled her feet in the water. She worked hard and played hard, and this being out of control was not what she liked in her life. She'd sworn long ago that she would be the one to call the shots. Yet here she was, totally out of her comfort zone, and the sensation creeping up her spine wasn't fear, or dismay, but delight.

Why?

She reclined back on the dock and closed her eyes. The sunlight hit her face, its fading heat still enough to help her relax. She was trapped here for the week. There was no way she would be stupid enough to try to get out of the bush alone, so she had two choices. Whine about it, or hop in with both feet. Have a great time with the guy, then take the memories with her when she left.

She needed a break right now anyway. With her partner retired, she had to train a new one, and she had a month's leave coming. Time to set some new goals for her life. Twenty-six, and already feeling like she might be alone forever.

But not this week. Whether he realized it or not, TJ had hit her right when she needed this most. She sat up and kicked the water, splashing and raising a ruckus. Life should be enjoyed, and she had every intention of enjoying it to the hilt for this week. The sun slipped behind the mountaintop, casting a shadow across the lake and she breathed in the clear air. It was definitely a place to make some memories.

TJ watched her, his wolf poking him to go to her side. She seemed so small and alone sitting on the dock, and he was a little worried he'd pushed it too hard bringing her here. Hopefully the next days would be enough for him to convince her he was a forever kind of guy.

When she threw back her head and laughed, splashing like a child, he had to fight back the urge to run and join her.

All his life he'd longed to have the kind of connection he'd seen in others of the pack. How it would work with him being a wolf and her human, he still didn't know, but there was no one else who had ever made him feel this way.

Groveling about to commence.

He approached slowly, but she heard him. Turning her body, she pulled her legs up and wrapped her arms around her knees. She smiled at him and the warmth hit him like a two-by-four between the eyes.

"You getting hungry?" he asked.

She nodded. "By the way, are you going to tell me where we are?"

"Northwest of Haines Junction, on one of the northern arms of Kluane Lake. The cabin is a friend's, and he and his wife have gone south visiting family."

"How did you get everything here? It's clean and stocked and everything."

"Shaun, the helicopter pilot. He came in earlier, brought supplies and cleaned up for us."

The streak of mischief lighting her face was slightly frightening. "You seemed to have brought a few supplies of your own."

He coughed. "About that... I didn't mean to presume, and it's totally up to you if we..."

Pam rose to her feet and stretched, and his mouth watered. Her breasts pressed against the front of her T-shirt, the muscles of her arms reflecting the glowing light of the setting sun. She stepped nearer.

"Don't presume, but I do like you. I'm pretty interested myself, as I think you could tell from the other night. So don't get all shy and shit on me. Do you want me?"

Oh my God. "More than you could possibly know."

She licked her lips as she checked him over. "Looks like we might have an interesting week ahead of us. Only your list of activities? I want to see what you've got planned. I wanted a northern experience, and you're going to give it to me, right?"

Oh yeah, he'd give her anything she wanted.

He held out his hand. "Supper first? Then we'll plan tomorrow?"

She took his fingers into hers and clasped them tightly.

Dishes were done, the fireplace crackled and TJ couldn't keep his eyes off her.

"Thanks for supper."

He snorted. "I should have warned you, I'm not that good a cook."

"Hey, mac and cheese with all the ketchup I wanted? What more is needed?" She held out her wine glass and he topped it up. "Your buddy Shaun did a fine job with the supplies."

He stared at her a little longer. The smooth sweep of her cheek, the way her hair hung over her skin and shone with the light. She was gorgeous and he ached for her.

"You want to play a game?" He needed something to distract him from stripping her and burying himself in her body before she was ready. Her scent filled the room, and he had to concentrate hard to stop from drooling.

"A game? Sure." She put down her wine glass and crawled into his lap, and he nearly swallowed his tongue.

"What...what are you doing?" *Holy shit.* She unbuttoned the top of his shirt and leaned in to press a kiss to his neck.

"Trying to decide what game to play."

It was hard to hear with the blood rushing past his ears en-route from leaving his brain to congregate in more southerly regions. When she sat up and stripped off her T-shirt, he squeezed his eyes shut tight, locking his fingers through the belt loops on her shorts. He was not going to rush her. She could set the pace.

"Hmm, I'd say strip poker, but I'm really bad at cards, so that wouldn't last very long." He didn't dare peek, but her hands were back on him. She finished the rest of his buttons and slipped the shirt from his shoulders. He leaned forward to let her maneuver the garment the rest of the way off, and his chest hit her breasts. Her naked, hot, bare breasts.

His eyes popped open. "Oh, sweet mercy, you're killing me."

"Why would you say that?" She cupped herself, rolling her nipples between thumb and forefinger, and stars floated in front of his vision.

"Pam, are you sure? We don't have to do this, not tonight."

That wasn't him talking. Some stranger had abducted him. *He* would have been touching her, smoothing her skin, reaching out to lap at the pale pink circles peaking her breasts. He wouldn't be stupid enough to try to slow her down, or heaven forbid, stop her from shifting slightly upward and bringing her nipple in contact with his lips.

Just a taste. He licked lightly and the tip hardened under his tongue. Her flavour rolled through him, intoxicating and rich. He closed his lips and sucked.

"Yes. Oh, yes." Pam dragged her fingers through his hair and held him close, and there was no stopping the train. He switched from side to side, feasting on her body, the crackle of the fire fading as her cries increased in volume. She was loud and vocal, and while he'd never had trouble making the ladies happy in bed, knowing what turned his mate on was the most awe-inspiring feeling he'd ever experienced.

He cupped her butt and stood, shuffling toward the bedroom as she latched onto his lips. Walking blind, he bumped into the doorframe a couple of times until he made it through and backed to the edge of the bed. He lowered her to the firm surface and stepped back to stare.

Her dark hair spread over the light-coloured comforter, her lips wet from their kisses, her bare torso enticing. She unsnapped her waist button and opened the zipper, and he couldn't breath. Could barely think as she wiggled out of her shorts and undies.

Naked.

Waiting.

His wolf howled with delight. His mate wanted him. Was waiting for him. He stepped closer and fell to his knees. One firm pull brought her hips to the end of the mattress. He opened her legs and kissed her intimately. She laughed, and it turned into a moan as he extended his tongue and licked her slit, separating her curls and finding her wet and ready.

His cock ached behind his clothing, but he was glad for the distraction. He wanted to make this special for her. Their first time, first of forever as far as he was concerned. He tasted her again, reveling in her gasps, the breathy moans escaping her throat as he circled her clit with his tongue.

When he slid a finger into her sheath and suckled at the same time, she cried out and came, her body responding far too quickly. It wasn't enough, not nearly enough pleasure. He refused to stop, holding her down when she wiggled. One hand stilled her hips as he continued to lick and suck, pumping two fingers into her core, massaging her sheath.

"You're killing me. Too sensitive, it's too much."

He lifted his head to soak in the sight. Her cheeks were flushed, her eyes glazed. She took a deep, shaky breath and his heart expanded. That response was because of him. Because of what he was doing to her.

"Never enough. I want you to come again before I sink into you. Before it's not my fingers filling you up, but my cock joining us together."

She screwed her eyes shut and hissed. Her pussy was wet and the intimate sounds of his fingers thrusting into her filled the air. When she came this time, it was with a contented sigh, and he dropped his head on her belly and shivered with how intensely satisfied it made him feel to please his mate.

He slowed his fingers, caressing the entrance to her body softly. Circling the delicate tissues as she continued to convulse under him. He rose and joined her, kissing her tenderly, rolling her to the side as she buried her hands in his hair.

Long breathless moments later she pulled back, stroking his cheek, her gaze darting over his face.

"Thank you, that was amazing."

"We're not done." He lowered his head and took her lips again. He couldn't get enough of her mouth, the scent and taste of her filling his head and making him crazy. She tugged on his pants, pushing the fabric over his hips, her soft hands caressing the bare skin of his butt. His cock touched her warm leg, and he shuddered, fighting for control.

"Lift up," she whispered, and then, sweet mercy, she had her hands on his cock and he was going to die. He nestled his face against her throat, soaking in every sensation—the scent of her skin, the aching pleasure in his balls as she somehow, from somewhere, rolled a condom onto his shaft.

He wished the damn thing were a million miles away. He wanted to take his mate, skin on skin. Needed to feel her wetness around him. Her warmth enclosing him, but he'd known that wouldn't work. So the condom it was, and even as he ached for what he couldn't have, she shifted under him, opening her legs, and the head of his cock breached her pussy.

"Take me." Pam arched against him and he slid in a tiny bit farther.

With pleasure. He slipped in slowly, savouring the sensation of her clasp around him until he was buried to the hilt. She was tight and wet and holy-fucking-moly nothing had ever felt like this before.

He stared into her big brown eyes. Anchored on his elbows, one on either side of her, their bodies joined together, a slow and seductive dance of pleasure. The hint of a smile appeared at the corner of her mouth, and he kissed it. Kissed his way across her cheek and back to her neck. He wanted to bite her so badly his gums ached. Wanted to mark her as his and make sure no matter what happened he would have that connection with her, but he couldn't. Not until she knew everything. Somewhere he found the strength to simply lick her jugular, ignoring the pounding pulse under his mouth. He concentrated on dragging his cock in and out of her sweet body.

Pam wrapped her legs around him, and on the next pass, he sank a little deeper and she made a little sound that made his balls tighten.

"So good. Oh yeah, right there." She swore a couple of times and he laughed.

"What's good, this?" He slid over her clit. It must have been sensitive from his earlier ministrations, and her eyes rolled back a little. "Yup, that's what I thought."

"Faster," she demanded, tugging with her feet against his ass.

He chuckled and dropped to suck on her nipples, nipping lightly with his teeth, soothing the rigid peaks with his tongue. "Slower."

He was going numb for the waist down, which, when added to how confused and crazy she made his mind, turned the whole situation a little cloudy and surreal. He didn't want it to end, didn't want to speed up, but the tingling ache at the base of his spine warned he wasn't going to last forever. He kissed her again, taking her mouth and commanding her attention. He plunged as deep as possible, pressing her against the bed so hard it squeaked, her breath rushing past his cheek as he reached down and slipped a hand between them.

"Come for me again. One more time. Squeeze me in that sweet pussy of yours until I can't stand it anymore."

He pressed on her clit in time with his thrusts. Pam clutched his neck in a death grip, and when she moaned out in pleasure, he closed his eyes and slammed in. Again and again as her body clutched him, waves convulsing around him. He hung on to his control by a thread. Then her hot mouth and seeking lips closed on his neck, and she bit him.

He exploded into her depths.

Chapter Six

Sorry guys, I didn't get anything useful out of Jared. TJ was very smart—all he told Jared was he planned on taking his vacation a little early and didn't want to leave the excursion in the lurch, could Jared fill in for a few days? He knows nothing more.

Find Shaun. He's the one who took them away. Check Granite Lake cabin, check the usual hangouts. I'm trapped taking care of this booking. When I find that boy I'm going to skin him alive. Robyn, you said you wanted a new rug for the living room, right?

Keil

Bliss.

Why had she never done this before? The totally decadent adoration of a slightly younger guy was awesome. Here she'd been going out with older men thinking that being more mature they would know their way around a girl's pink parts better, but TJ? Whoa Nelly, the guy had talented fingers.

Even now he was using them to her best advantage. Last night had rocked, and she couldn't quite remember when she'd fallen asleep. Somewhere between their third and fourth tumble on the bed, things got blurry, but the drag of his hands down her back as he massaged her naked body this morning was very clear.

Bliss.

Or had she thought that already?

He pressed harder, his thumbs sinking into the tight muscles in her lower back and she groaned. "Oh yeah, right there."

"Hmm, sleeping beauty awakes. I seem to remember you saying that a lot last night."

"Oh yeah?"

"And the 'right there'. You're very vocal in bed. I like that." He kissed her cheek and lay next to her, the warmth of his bare skin covering her in lieu of the quilt.

"Don't see any good reason to be shy."

He watched her with the strangest expression on his face.

She leaned up on one elbow. "What?"

"How do you feel?"

"Well fucked."

He frowned and stared in silence for a minute.

"Am I supposed to feel something else? You're a seriously good lover, TJ. I'm happy as a clam, or I would be if you'd get back to what you were doing a minute ago." She caught a flash of sadness in his eyes, but as curious as it made her, deep introspection before she'd brushed her teeth was not in the books. "Hey, did you tell me there's a shower?"

He kissed her nose before sitting up and resuming his magic touch on her body.

"Massage first. You can shower while I'm cooking breakfast. The water heater is a rapid-fire system and I turned on the pump last night. With a lake full of water and the propane generator, you can have as long a shower as you want."

"This place is not nearly as rustic as it appears at first glance."

"Only the best for you."

She laughed. "So glad you had my comfort in mind when you shanghaied me." She lay back to enjoy what the day would hold.

They sat overlooking the lake while a delicious sensation of fatigue stole through her limbs. Private excursions by Kidnappers R Us for the win. "Other than warning you I'm taking over the cooking, this day has been incredible. I loved the canoeing, and the hike to the lookout was fabulous."

"Sorry about the grilled cheese sandwiches at lunch."

"Hey, a little carbon is supposed to be good for the system, right? Clears it out."

TJ smiled at her as he touched her hair. He'd been doing that all day long. Stroking her cheek, holding her hand. Even with him acting like some kind of weird stalker, she couldn't muster any concern. It was all so innocent, and tender.

"I'm very thankful you've been so understanding about me...well..."

"The kidnapping? Forget it. I tried to get upset, but somewhere at about the fifteenth orgasm all my ability to be freaked out seemed to float away."

"You haven't come that many times."

She laughed softly. "Well, then, you'd better get busy, hadn't you?"

He moved closer, wrapped an arm behind her and let her lean against him. "Tonight. Right now, enjoy the view. I know I am."

"You're not even looking around." Pam flushed. The man never seemed to take his eyes off her. "You're staring again."

"I know."

"It's very flattering."

TJ tugged her head against his chest and she relaxed, letting him support her weight as they watched the sun approach the top of the mountain. Under her ear his heart pulsed evenly, the solid beat lulling her into a lazy state.

"You think you'd like to live up north?" he asked.

She'd thought about it, but moving wasn't practical. "It's pretty, but my job is down south. I need to get ready to train a new partner."

"Partner?"

"RCMP, remember? My partner retired and I'll need to go start the process again." She sighed. "Damon was awesome. I miss him a lot."

A strange choking cough shook TJ. "Damon?"

"Yeah. We were inseparable. Even on the coldest nights he warmed me up." TJ tensed under her, and Pam turned toward him. His face was bright red and his lips were moving, but no sound was coming out. "You okay?"

He shook his head and cleared his throat a few times. "I'll be fine. I've never had a woman tell me about an old lover like this, while we're—"

"Lover?" *What the hell? Oh shit.* A laugh burst out. By the time she'd regained control, her stomach was sore and she was gasping for air. It didn't help that every time she looked at TJ his expression set her off again.

"Sorry...don't mean to be rude. Oh my God, you're kidding me. Didn't you know? Damon was my partner, but he's a dog."

"That's my opinion for sure."

"No, seriously, a German Shepherd. I'm a dog handler for the Royal Canadian Mounted Police. Narcotics division, and I double in Search and Rescue when needed."

"You're a dog handler?" He collapsed back onto the blanket, his arms flung out to the side. "Oh man, I am never going to live this one down."

Pam crawled nearer, resting her head on his chest. There was something very comfortable about the position. "I know, it's a bit of a surprise, but I'm not sure why you think it's such an odd job. It's been a great way to be involved in the RCMP and still be able to enjoy working with animals. I debated training as a vet, but with one thing and another, it didn't work out."

TJ rolled her, leaning close to nuzzle her neck, and the rising anticipation she was coming to expect around him seized her again. He spoke quietly, the brush of air from his lips teasing her ear. "I think it's a fabulous job, and I bet you are completely awesome. All the dogs must have contests to figure out who gets you as their partner."

"Goof."

"Just saying..."

She chuckled then broke into a huge yawn. What an amazing day. TJ tangled his fingers in her hair to stroke and pet her, and she wrapped her arms around his neck to encourage him closer.

He took the hint and kissed her. Slow and thorough. Damn, he tasted good. It was like he knew exactly what kind of mood she was in. Tired from their busy day, she felt dreamy and soft, and that's how he kissed her. He pulled back and his eyes sparkled, the dark centers mesmerizing. "As pleasurable as this is, I need to make sure I tied the canoe properly. I have a sneaky suspicion I forgot, and I don't want to have to go for a swim tomorrow to find it."

"You want me to come with you?"

"You can, or you can stay here. I'll only be a minute."

She waved him off as another yawn escaped. She lay back on the blanket. Oh yeah, she was totally into this holiday. Six more days? They should think about getting an extension.

She covered her eyes with her arm and breathed in deeply. The clean air filled her lungs with a fresh energy. She wondered what new tricks they could get up to tonight. Maybe make love in front of the fire.

Something inside paused. Since when did she call it making love? Sex was sex. You took care of your partner, had some fun then moved on.

A rustling in the nearby trees made her sit up, and she watched carefully for signs of what made the noise. They hadn't spotted any wildlife yet, and that was one thing she hoped to change before heading home.

She stood to have a better view. The lower limbs of a bush wiggled. Something small. The sound of sniffing reached her ears and she hesitated.

That didn't sound like a deer or a caribou or some other four-legged vegetarian. The head that popped out from the forest was brown washed with streaks of grey. One plate-sized paw followed another and Pam froze in terror.

Bear.

Oh my God, what was she supposed to do? She racked her brain for the training session she'd taken on bear encounters, but it had been a long time ago. *Stay still. It can't see me if I don't move.*

No, wait—that's what you're supposed to do for a T-Rex.

There was still a fair distance between her and the bear, so she took a cautious step backward. The animal's head pivoted in her direction and it sniffed harder.

Pam clenched her teeth together to stop them from chattering.

The animal reared on its hind legs, scenting the air. It snorted at her, twice.

She took another step backward and spoke softly. "Go away. I'm human. I'm not interesting at all. Oh damn, *damn, damn,* TJ, this is a rotten time to be out strolling." Sneaking a peek over her shoulder to see if there was any action by the lake tempted her, but that would have required taking her eyes off the bear and *that* was physically impossible.

The beast wavered, its upper body rocking from side to side for a second before it suddenly dropped to all fours, and with a nerve-racking grumble, it rushed her. She shouted, adrenaline flashing through her veins. She looked around frantically for a stick or a rock or anything to defend herself, but there was nothing at hand, and besides, her limbs were frozen in terror.

A blur of silver fur flew past her from behind. She stumbled back and swore as she identified a canine-like body darting at the bear. Her attacker jerked to a stop, and snarled, its teeth gnashing together before spinning around. It disappeared into the bush with a crash, the wolf hard on its heels. A loud howl rang out as her protector paused at the tree line before pacing over to sit a short distance from her feet.

Pam wrapped her arms around herself to stop the shaking from taking over even as she stared at the animal.

How in the world?

"Wolfie?"

Chapter Seven

Keil

Granite Lake is empty. There's no sign of him at any of the pack's summer retreats. We even checked the old-timer's trapline cabins and came up blank. As for Shaun, he did a supply run up north to Old Crow then parked the chopper and said he was taking a week-long vacation. The locals saw him head into the bush with a backpack. Looks like he's the only one who knows where Pam and TJ are, and he's making sure no Alpha can contact him and order him to spill the beans.

I discovered a couple of the other single guys in the pack put together a food package for TJ. Seems he called in favours from all his buddies. All they can say is TJ asked for help and no one turns him down.

BTW, Maggie texted. She said you don't have to worry about Pam suing us, but you might not get a chance to skin TJ. Pam is very capable of handing out her own chastisement. Did you remember she's an RCMP? You're going to die when you hear the division she works in.

Robyn

Shit.

Shit.

Pam was totally going to kill him. And after that Keil was going to rip off his fur and use him for trimming coats. Halfway back from the lake he'd spotted the bear rearing before her. It was probably just trying to figure out what she was—bears had rotten eyesight—but he wasn't sure Pam knew it simply wanted to catch her scent. And while there was no reason for it to really attack, he couldn't risk her misunderstanding if it made a false rush forward. His wolf demanded he take action, and before he knew it he had stripped, shifting as he ran to convince ol' Bruin to hightail it off for a different patch of berries.

TJ moved slowly toward Pam who stared around in confusion. She yelled his name out a few times. "TJ! You ass, get your butt up here."

She was a freaking dog handler. How was he supposed to talk to her? For the millionth time he wished they were completely mated like full-blood wolves. That he could talk to her mind and have her hear his voice.

"Okay, you look like the pet wolf I met at Maggie's. But that's flipping impossible. Stay."

He froze. Anything to make her more comfortable.

"Shit, you're not supposed to be trained. How did you get here? Come." She snapped her fingers and TJ trotted to her side as she continued to call his name out loud in the direction of the lake.

His internal debate continued. If he ran into the trees and doubled back behind the cabin, he could shift and pretend to have been in there the whole time. Except that would explain his absence, but not the presence of the "wolfie", and it would be a lie.

He didn't want to lie to her. Didn't want to keep up the deception. He ached to tell her everything, and following at her heels as she ran to the cabin, he made his decision. He was going to show her.

Maybe it was too soon. But...they'd hit it off, right? Surely it would be better to be honest now instead of coming clean later and having the lies held over his head. She pushed open the door and searched the cabin.

"TJ, where in the hell are you?"

He blocked her path when she would have left the cabin, nudging her instead toward the couch.

"Stop it, I need to find TJ."

He forced his body weight against her legs to make her move the direction he wanted, and suddenly sharp pain radiated out from his ear, followed by his throat, as she put him into a chokehold.

"Stay."

Okay, enough of her ordering him around like a dog. He hesitated for all of two seconds before shifting back into his human form.

Pam's heart rate hovered around three hundred beats per minute. It had shot up there when the bear appeared and pretty much stayed at that level all the way until the damn dog blocked her path. Fuck this, she needed to get out of the building and no animal was going to stop her. Of course, feeling the fur under her elbow change to human skin and discovering she clutched the ear of a naked TJ did things to her blood pressure she was pretty sure were dangerous.

She released him and slammed back into the door. TJ rose to his feet and stepped away from her, his hands held out non-threateningly.

"What. The hell. Just. Happened," she shouted. He cringed. Okay, maybe she was a few decibels over the safety levels, but...*fuck.*

"I can explain."

Pam gasped for air. She wasn't sure if she was going to throw up or laugh. Her stomach rolled a little more, and she would have closed her eyes but she wanted to make sure she knew where he was at all times.

"Start now. Make it snappy."

TJ glanced down at his naked body. "Can I pull on some clothes?"

She nodded. Even while freaking out she found him distractingly attractive. He turned and disappeared into the bedroom they'd shared last night, his naked butt teasing her.

He'd turned into a wolf. That wasn't possible.

He returned and dug into the cooler, poured a glass of something and gestured for her to sit on the couch. She had to peel herself off the door.

"You planning on..." She couldn't think what to accuse him of. He'd turned into a freaking wolf.

He held out the glass.

"Orange juice. The calories are supposed to be good for people who have had a shock. Damn it, Pam, I'm really sorry. I didn't mean to spill the beans this way. The bear wasn't going to hurt you. I mean, I know that must have been freaky to have him run at you like that, but that's called a bluff, because this time of year he'd be more interested in the berries. He just wanted to scare you off, but I still needed to make sure you were safe, and I know it's a lot to take in—" He slammed his lips together and motioned with the glass. "Please, you'll feel better."

She sat across from him and sipped the juice. The ringing in her ears slowly died down so she could hear again. He smiled when she placed the empty glass on the table.

He'd changed into a wolf.

That was actually extraordinary. Totally amazing. Incredible and frightening at the same time.

"So this thing you plan on telling me is that in your secret life you're a pet wolf?"

He burst out laughing, then stopped abruptly. "Sorry, but oh my God, that's funny. No, I am a wolf but not a pet. I mean, I'm a wolf and a human, but it's not like the scary 'moonlight makes me mad and I rip out throats' or anything. Really."

Pam resisted clutching her legs. "Werewolf?"

TJ tilted his head from side to side. "Kinda? But more like I'm a human and I can also change into a wolf. There's no in-between stage."

She shivered involuntarily. He leaned forward as if he planned to come and join her, and she held up a hand. "Don't. Just...don't push it too fast, okay? I think I might be past the point I'm going to fall into a dead faint, but you need to give me some time."

He sat back and folded his hands in his lap, the hopeful expression he wore making her snort. She rose and paced to the door.

"You're not leaving, are you?" He sounded panicked and she took pity on him. She'd never figure this out if she ran.

"No, but I need to move. Tell me more."

"Okay, except...there isn't much more to tell. I can change into a wolf. Always have been able to, since I was about twelve. Umm, there's a whole bunch of us, and we—"

Oh my God. "Maggie. Does she know about this?"

TJ hesitated. "Pam, I'm going to be completely honest with you but you have to promise not to freak out."

A laugh escaped—a little thin and quivery around the

edges. "I don't think I can promise that, but I'll try."

"Maggie knows. She's always known because she's also a wolf. She married a wolf. My brother is a wolf. His wife is a wolf. Heck, ninety percent of Haines have the wolf gene, either full blood or half. Together we belong to the Granite Lake pack, and we've got a kind of government and hierarchy and, well, it's complicated at times, but usually it's pretty cool."

Pam stopped her pacing and leaned on the wall for a minute to calm herself. Everything she'd ever known as reality was slipping away and somehow she had to make sense of it.

Her best friend was able to change into a wolf and never told her? The huge gorgeous men she'd seen at the wedding were all wolf shifters? Unbelievable, and yet it had to be true. Pain swelled inside, not so much fear, but a lack of certainty. Sadness at what she thought was truth being ripped away.

She turned to TJ. Concern was written all over him, in the tightness of his shoulders, the expression on his face. He shook his head slowly.

"I'm sorry. I didn't want to hurt you like this. Please, please don't be scared. I'll do anything in my power to make it better. Anything. Ask as many questions as you want, I swear I'll tell you everything. The only thing I won't do is let anyone harm my family." He stood slowly and held out his arms.

Insane. From one moment to the next she was doing everything wrong. He kidnapped her, and she laughed and had sex with him. Now he revealed he was a wild beast at times, and she was powerless to stop herself from stepping into his arms and accepting his embrace.

She clutched him hard, wrapping her arms around his torso and resting her head on his chest. He rubbed her back in slow, even circles. Under her ear his heart thumped, the consistent pulse reassuring and steady. He didn't say anything—just let her soak in his warmth, the comfort of his presence.

In the midst of her rocking world, he gave her balance.

She drew a deep breath, unsteady and ragged, and he swore. "You're killing me. It's going to be okay. Please, trust me. Nothing bad will happen to you. I'll make sure everything works out." He lifted her chin and stared at her with compassion, his pupils huge.

She tried to smile. "It's getting easier to accept, but I am so going to kick Maggie's butt the next time I see her."

He leaned toward her, his intentions clear, and she held her breath. Did she want to kiss him?

"Pam?"

More than wanted to, needed to. She lifted her mouth and he kissed her carefully. With a gentle stroke he brushed away the tears that had filled her eyes as her world was thrown into chaos. He traced a finger down her cheek. "Maggie has a story to tell you, but it's hers to share, not mine. I will tell you she's always said you were her best friend in the whole world and she loves you a ton. She never kept secrets to hurt you."

She nodded. "Any other bombs you need to drop on me? Like is drinking the Yukon water going to make me able to shift or anything?"

Pain flashed across his face.

"No, afraid it doesn't work that way." He kissed her forehead. "Unfortunately there is one more thing I need to tell you, and it's probably going to be another doozy of a revelation. You want it before or after supper?"

He released her and she went to the sink to splash her face with water. More mysteries? Her heart couldn't take much more.

"Is it really important?"

He nodded. "You should sit down."

Oh shit. "That bad, eh?"

"I'll promise to turn into my wolf afterward and you can twist my ear again if it makes you feel better."

She chuckled. "Goof."

He sighed mightily. "Hold on to your sense of humour, you might need it."

She sat and he sank to the floor at her feet. His expression was serious and concerned, so different than what she'd seen in him over the past days.

"Hey, where's that lighthearted guy who makes me smile gone? You can turn into a wolf. It's not the end of the world, not unless you give me fleas. I hate having to deal with flea infestations."

He took her hands in his and brought them to his lips, kissing her knuckles tenderly.

"No fleas...but something a little more permanent. I mentioned we've got a kind of government? My big brother, Keil, is the head of the Granite Lake pack."

"Really? That's kinda cool. Why is that an issue?"

"Well, it's not, but he's the Alpha since he's the strongest wolf around. There're these unspoken rules that happen in a pack, based on our wolves. Keil and his wife, Robyn, you remember her? They're the top of the heap. Well, one of the other things our wolves decide is..."

He shook his head slowly and brought her hand to his ear. "Here. You may as well grab on now."

How could she stay angry around him? She laughed and leaned forward to give him a kiss, smoothing her fingers through his hair. The sensation distracted her. "That's what your hair reminded me of."

"What?"

She stroked again, reveling in the softness. So soothing to the touch. Something about caressing, being close to TJ made her happy inside, lighting all the dark corners. "Your fur. The night you slept with me in your wolf form I fell asleep stroking you. That's what your hair feels like. So soft."

He shivered. "God, you keep touching me like that and I'm never going to get this out."

She stilled her hands. "Just tell me. It's not like you're going to shock the daylights out of me."

"We're mates."

She paused. "Sure. We're best buds. Whatever you say. Now tell me the rest of the news because getting freaked out seems to have made me hungry."

He shook his head wildly. "No, you don't understand. Mates, as in the way a wolf takes a mate. You know dogs, you must know a little bit about wolves. We have a lot of the characteristics of wolves, and just like there's an alpha and an omega wolf, our wolves pick our mate and they pick them for life. You, me. My wolf picked you."

TJ stared into the fire. It was far too early to be getting up and way too late to still be awake. After his little life-changing revelation, Pam had snatched together the fixings for a sandwich then retreated to the bedroom to "get some space to think". He'd settled in to wait and see what the verdict would be.

He'd screwed everything up. Everything.

Crap, why had he imagined, even for a moment, that

hauling Pam into the bush against her will would make anything easier? Time alone, right. He poked the logs and watched the sparks fly upward in protest. That's what he had now, time completely alone. Just him and the couch, which was lumpy and uncomfortable, and he'd sleep on it for the next week without a single complaint if Pam would give them a chance.

He'd sleep on it forever if she asked him to.

The floorboards creaked in the bedroom and he stood in a rush, staring at the door in the hopes she'd come out. The freaky part was he sensed where she was—and what she was feeling—just a little. His brother had explained once how the connection between him and his mate Robyn worked. While this wasn't as strong as Keil had described, it was vivid enough to give TJ a teeny tiny fraction of hope to cling to.

Maybe there would be more to their mate connection than he'd dreamed possible.

When she'd barricaded herself in the bedroom, she'd been royally pissed at him, and he'd taken it in stride. It was the confusion that followed and the tears shortly after that had him on the verge of ignoring her request and breaking down the door, because he knew he could comfort her.

Needed to comfort her.

Now he stood as still as possible, trying to figure out the way to connect with her. They had made love—it had to count for something. In spite of the damn condom, there *had* to be a bond to help them make it through this rough beginning. She wasn't sleeping, and she wasn't mad. An even calm greeted him and now he was the one confused. Calm? After all he'd thrown at her in the past couple days?

Holy shit, she was the most intriguing person he'd ever met and right there in that moment all his doubts washed away.

If he had to turn his back on his family to be with her, so be it. He'd move south, find a job. He'd still have to turn wolf every now and then, but he'd find a way to do that wherever she was. He'd court her properly, and eventually she'd accept him, if not as a lover, then as a friend.

It would kill a part of him, but being with her would be worth it.

The door creaked open an inch and their eyes met. He bit his lip. *Let her call the shots.* Her lashes were still wet from her earlier tears and something tore at his belly. His resolve wavered. Okay, not comforting his mate? Sucked donkey balls.

"Can we talk?"

TJ nodded so rapidly his vision blurred. Pam opened the door wider. He hauled his gaze off where the oversized T-shirt she wore barely covered the tops of her thighs. This was not the time to get distracted, even though his mate made his knees weak with longing.

"Here's the deal. I know you're not lying about being a wolf. I saw it."

Promising opening.

"I also believe you're insane, in the nicest possible way."

Umm, that doesn't sound as good. Begging commences now... "Tell me what you want me to do that would fix this for you. If you want, I'll shift to my wolf and run until I find a place with a phone. It will take me a while to organize, but I'm sure I can find a way to get you home early."

She snorted. "You're not getting out of this that easy, buster." Pam stalked to his side and grabbed him by the collar. She eyed him up and down and his fading hope flickered back to life. "You promised me seven days of wilderness adventures, with lots of hot monkey sex thrown in."

"What are you saying?" He could barely breathe.

"Well, other than you have to offer hot *wolfie* sex, I'm making you stick to your commitment. But you've now got an additional challenge. You say we're 'mates'. Fine. You have until the end of the week to prove it."

Chapter Eight

The past couple of hours had been sheer agony as Pam fought with herself to pick the right thing to do next.

Step one. Get abducted by a virtual stranger? Check.

Two. Completely forget all rules of safety and have sex with said kidnapper? Check.

Three. Have the guy she was developing suspiciously strong feelings for turn into a wild animal in front of her then suggest they were meant to be together for the rest of their lives? Once you put a check in that box, what the hell were you supposed to do for a follow-up performance?

But it was true. She'd seen him change—it was a reality she had to face, no matter how much her mind rebelled at the thought. Shrieking or wailing wouldn't move this situation forward.

Logic was always the best thing to fall back on. Logic, and an oversized baseball bat.

TJ rocked on his feet, his hands twisting together until he deliberately shoved them into his pockets. "You don't want me to get us back to Haines?"

She shook her head. "If we go back now that doesn't answer any more of my questions, does it? I suspect once we reach civilization we're going to have a few other issues to deal with."

TJ's cringe said it all. Yup—that hierarchy he'd mentioned in passing—she bet he was up the creek without a paddle in their books right now. His big brother was in charge? Thinking back to the way the whole group had worked her at the wedding ceremony, she suspected there were a few well-greased wheels in play. Who knew what weird rules TJ had broken? Someone was undoubtedly on the lookout for them even now.

But this was *her* life and she would be the one to make the decisions. Not some well-meaning older brother, or even Maggie, although Pam suspected her BFF could answer a few questions.

In spite of the adrenaline rush that had spiked through her for most of the evening and night, or maybe because of it, an enormous yawn overtook her.

TJ spoke quietly. "Let's call it a night and tomorrow I'll do my best to show you...well, I'll show you how this works. But anytime you have questions, you ask. I promise I won't keep anything from you."

"Holding your tongue doesn't seem to be the issue, TJ."

"Sorry, very true."

Pam covered her mouth as another yawn hit her. Bed. It was past two and definitely time for some sleep. She turned and paced into the bedroom. The chill in the air encouraged her to dive under the quilt. She pounded the pillows a few times trying to settle in comfortably when she realized she was alone. She sat up to see TJ staring at her from where he still stood in the living room.

"Aren't you coming?"

"You want me to sleep with you?" He dragged a hand through his hair. "Okay. I mean, I want to join you, but..."

He walked forward slowly, dropping into a crouch beside

the bed. His long fingers carefully stroked back a strand of hair from her forehead and his touch sent a shiver through her.

"Pam. You want me to prove we're mates, then here's the first demonstration. I think getting into bed with you right now would be a mistake. You're still in shock and while there's this incredible physical pull between us because we are mates, if anything happens sexually you're going to regret it.

"Still, I can feel how much you need to be comforted right now, and so here's the best I can do."

He kissed her forehead tenderly then walked to the opposite side of the bed. He turned his back and stripped off his shirt, tossing it on a nearby chair. The pale light from the dying fire leaked in through the open doorway, brushing delicate highlights along the solid ridges of his body. Pam sucked for air. He was simply gorgeous. The way he moved made her hot and bothered, even when he wasn't turning sexual attention on her.

There was a huge grin on his face as he pivoted and sank to his knees. "The way you're looking at me is giving me a thrill. I'll shift back when you need me in the morning."

Though she watched as carefully as possible, she couldn't figure out how he did it. One minute he was a human, stooping low to the ground, the next a beautiful wolf leapt onto the bed beside her. He batted her with his head, blowing warm air from his nostrils as he nuzzled her neck.

Something simply amazing—followed by something normal. It was so TJ. "Goof."

He licked her cheek from jawbone to temple, a long slow drag that made her giggle. As one they settled, her arms wrapped around him, her fingers tangled in his fur to hold him close.

A tight ball of fear she'd been denying slipped out from inside her belly and unraveled.

How had he known? She'd needed to take charge and make this work. And yeah, she had the major hots for him. But this? She stroked his fur and he let loose a rumble, soft and low, in his throat. He radiated calmness, cautiously rolling to avoid bumping her too hard.

Closing her eyes, she was surrounded by a strong sensation of peace. His rhythmic heartbeat felt perfect under her hands as she fell asleep stroking him.

TJ was still in wolf form when they woke, and his enthusiastic good-morning kisses made her laugh until her stomach hurt. Her heart ached a little since that's how Damon used to greet her—with a wet tongue-lashing that had her scrambling for cover as he chased her around the tangled bed sheets.

Damn it, her new boyfriend reminded her of her dog. This couldn't be good.

She pushed him back enough she could sit up. He rested his chin on her thigh, big beautiful eyes staring up unblinking. She'd slept like a rock, his warm furry body pressed against her side, comforting and reassuring.

"Good morning, TJ."

He tilted his head to the side, his eyes sparkling at her. One ear wiggled and she swore he sighed with contentment. Damn, he was cute. "Dibs on the shower, then you can tell me what you've got planned for today."

TJ jumped off the bed and headed out the open door, leaving her alone in the room. She stripped off her sleep shirt and grabbed her things.

Mates. Werewolves. The calm, contented feeling she'd

woken to dissipated a little. How come she hadn't screamed and run away after waking up with a wolf in her bed?

Because it felt right?

The shower wasn't hot enough to wash away the rest of her unease, no matter how long she stayed in. Still, she'd offered TJ time to prove his point. Not that she had much choice about getting out of the wilderness without his help. When her fingers and toes grew wrinkled, she abandoned the water to face what the day would hold.

She rubbed a towel over her hair as she joined him at the kitchen table.

The toasted bagels were only slightly burnt. A fully human TJ poured her a cup of coffee and passed her the sugar container, his damp hair sticking up in spikes.

"Where did you shower?"

He pointed out the window. "In the lake."

Pam shivered. "You're kidding. The water is freezing."

"It's too cold for me in my human form, but my wolf doesn't mind a bit."

She took a long pull at her coffee, letting the heat of it wash over her. It may be a handy solution—having two forms like that—but she was grateful it had been him in the lake and not her.

He handed her a note pad. "We've all got in the habit of carrying paper around for those times we need to talk with Robyn and our sign language isn't adequate. While you were showering, I jotted down a few notes to distract me."

"Distract you?"

His gaze rolled down one side of her and up the other, and suddenly the room grew a whole lot warmer. "You were naked in the shower. Imagining you in there..."

Their eyes met and Pam swallowed around the bit of bagel stuck in her throat. Oh lordy, what had she gotten herself into? She stared at him, the dark pools of his eyes enticing her to dive in.

He nudged the notepad and broke the connection. "As per orders, I've got adventure activities planned for each day, but I've added to them. This list is the things that are normal for wolf mates to experience around each other. I thought we could work our way through some of them—sort of see how things go, and still get in the activities you signed up for originally."

He leaned forward and took her hand, his expression shifting from flirtatious to contrite. "I want to say one more time I'm really sorry I didn't ask you straight out if you wanted to get involved with me. I should have done things differently."

Wow. An unasked-for apology from a guy? Pam sat for a minute not sure what to say. "Okay."

She glanced at the paper. He'd drawn five circles on the page, overlapping them in the middle like a malformed daisy. Paired words filled each circle.

Mental link

Chemical attraction

Physical connection

Emotional attachment

Complementary interests

Pam hesitated. He was taking this damn seriously. "Chemical attraction? Isn't that the same thing as physical connection?"

TJ shook his head. "Not at all. One leads to the other, but I can assure you they are very different." He brushed the back of

211

his knuckles against her cheek before tucking her hair behind her ear. "This one might be hard to prove—heck they're all going to be tough, but this one might be the most wolfish. I'm guessing a bit, since I only know what I've been told about wolves' experiences. You being human..." He shrugged.

"So you don't know exactly what you're trying to prove?"

His eyes flashed. "Oh, I know exactly what I'm going to prove. That you and I belong together, without any doubt whatsoever."

Pam pushed back her chair slightly, feeling caged by his intensity. She grabbed the notepad and held it between them, dragging air into her lungs to try and calm the blood racing through her.

"Okay, chemical. In short that means? What?"

TJ took a slow, deep inhalation and moaned. "I am never going to be able to do that without getting hard. Okay—what it means is you smell right. I'm not talking about your perfume or your soap, but you." He closed his eyes and gripped the table tightly. "Just the smell of you makes me go weak-kneed. It makes me want to pick you up, carry you to bed and make love to you for hours."

Pam shivered, erotic images flashing in her mind.

He opened his eyes. "But it also makes me want to sit beside you for hours and listen to you tell me about your favourite food, and your day at work, and stories about when you were growing up."

Her stomach clenched before she deliberately relaxed it. No way he wanted to hear that kind of crap.

"So it's different from seeing someone at a bar or a dance club and getting turned on? Or for that matter, watching Gerard Butler in a movie and feeling the dire need to jump him?"

He rolled his eyes. "What is it with you chicks and that guy? No, not quite the same thing. More like—what would you do if you met him in person?"

She laughed. "Probably freeze."

"Right, and when we met, you wanted to...?"

She thought back to before the wedding. To the almost overwhelming desire to get to know him more intimately. "So we like how each other smells. I don't know if that's enough to prove anything to me."

TJ sat back and sipped his juice. "As long as you agree there is something—magnetic—between us."

She nodded slowly. That much she would confess to. It would also explain why no matter what insane thing he did, she responded the wrong way.

TJ tugged the notepad from her fingers. "Eat, the day is wasting. That's not the item on our agenda for today anyway."

Pam blinked in surprise. "It's not?"

"Nope." He topped up her coffee and raised his mug in a toast. "To working our way through the mate list."

Hide and go seek. She was playing hide and go seek in the Yukon bush with a werewolf. Pam tucked her legs a little closer to her body and made sure nothing was sticking out.

They'd spent the morning hiking to an abandoned miner's cabin and poking around for artifacts. After lunch he'd casually proposed this game, and now she sat in the branches of a tree, her body pressed against the trunk. TJ walked straight toward her like she'd left a trail of breadcrumbs for him to follow. He grinned at her and held out a hand.

"You need to work harder at this or I'm going to think

you're not trying."

"You're cheating. You've got lupine senses, don't you, even in your human form?" There had to be a reason he'd found her so quickly. The last *five* times she'd hidden.

TJ shook his head. "Well, I can smell you, but I can also feel where you are. It's like I told you, there's a mental link between us, and I'm following that." She pushed off the branch and he caught her, her body settling against his, warm and comfortable as she wrapped her arms around his neck.

"Fine. You can find me in a snowstorm. That's a cool trick."

"Hey, don't think this is a one-way street. I think you'll be able to do it as well."

He placed her on the grassy area outside the cabin yet refused to let her out of his arms.

"You planning on proving the physical connection right now?"

He flashed a grin. "No, but you wait. When we get kinky in bed, I'll know what you want. How hard, how fast." One hand skimmed her shoulder and down her spine, coming to rest on the small of her back. Intimate. The airy touch of his caress sent a tingling sensation racing up her body and her nipples tightened involuntarily. TJ spoke, his voice deep and husky. "Of course that means I can totally tease you."

Oh my God, do it now. The need to offer herself up on a silver platter was instinctive, and somewhat frightening. Time to retreat. She pressed her hands to his chest to separate them enough she could think. "Two-way street, bud? Be careful there, I might have to write you out a ticket."

He cupped her chin with his free hand. His grasp firmed until she lifted her gaze to meet his. "Don't. Don't hide behind jokes right now."

Pam closed her eyes and waited. His warm breath caressed her cheek as he brought their bodies back in contact.

"You look beautiful in the sunlight."

She opened her eyes just as he brushed his lips against hers. His dark lashes fluttered against her skin. She stroked her tongue into his mouth, no longer fighting the delightful sensations that streaked through her body.

They stood there, kissing slowly, hands gently exploring each other's bodies—Pam lost all track of time and slipped into a dreamy place where there were no issues hanging over her head. No need to discover if fairytales really could come true.

When they pulled apart, his smile warmed her through and through. "Well, that's not what I had planned, but I'll certainly take it. Stop distracting me. Your turn to hunt. No peeking while I hide."

Pam not only closed her eyes, she covered her face with her hands, like a child afraid they would be tempted to cheat. She didn't want to have any clue which direction he was headed. No chance she could pretend this was a fair test when it wasn't. She hummed quietly to cover any accidental sounds he might make that would give her a direction to head. Inspiration hit and she counted out loud.

"...ten, eleven, twelve...I hope you're hiding well because if I find you standing out in the open somewhere you have to buy me a crab dinner or something....seventeen, eighteen...or a case of beer, I could really go for a cold drink...twenty-three, twenty-four, twenty-five...ready or not, you must be caught."

She opened her eyes and took a long look around. The sun sparkled on the surface of the lake across from her, the tiny ripples from the whispering breeze creating a kaleidoscope of colour and light. Out by the cabin, the porch swing shifted slowly and she watched for a moment, but it sped up, didn't slow. The wind again, not TJ brushing it. She examined the bush, but other than natural shaking and trembling in the leaves she could see no clear hint of where TJ was hiding.

"Okay, I'll give you this much, you've hidden well. Now..."

The usual procedure would be to divide the area into sectors and methodically work her way through them. She paused. This wasn't supposed to be like a usual search, right? If they were mates, she should be able to sense him. She sniffed the air then laughed. No, she wasn't the one with the wolf nose.

She was still chuckling when she felt it. Almost a...lightness in the air, a sense of emotion brushing past her. TJ was pleased. Admiring her? She pressed a hand to her chest. It wasn't just her imagination. She closed her eyes once more and covered her ears. The wind in the trees faded away and all sound stilled, but the sensation increased. Oh my God, she *could* feel something. She twirled and ran for the cabin. The pounding of her footfalls as she raced up the stairs echoed off the low roof and she jerked open the door.

Disappointment hit her hard. She'd fully expected to find TJ on the couch. She'd felt sure he was there. Sitting comfortably, waiting for her.

Again, a tug. Like strings attached inside her heart.

She paced the cabin in confusion. He was supposed to be here.

"TJ, where are you?"

The sensation refused to go away. She checked under the bed, in the shower stall. Stepping outside, she kicked a rock in frustration before a flash of inspiration made her curse.

"You turkey." She raced around the back of the cabin to where the woodpile was stacked into a rough façade of a staircase. She scrambled to the top where it was level with the lightly inclined roof of the attached storage lean-to, and stared at TJ. He lay flat on his back on a thick blanket, grinning at her.

"Hey."

Deep satisfaction stole over her as she cautiously made her way to his side. "Hey, yourself. You got up here pretty damn quick."

His shit-eating grin grew larger. "And it took you oh-so-long to find me, didn't it?"

Holy crap, he was right. In the midst of the hunt, she'd lost grasp of the fact she had found him. Had known where he was. "Wow."

TJ patted the blanket. "How did you do it?"

Pam settled next to him, nestling into his arms. "I'm not completely sure. It's like I knew. But, it's not possible..."

He nuzzled at her temple. "Hmm, you just proved it is." His lips descended slowly to press, warm and soft, against her jawbone. He snuck his fingers into her hair and brought their mouths together, and she couldn't be bothered to try to figure out why she'd known where he was. She'd known. Score one for the mating list. Bring on the sex.

She rolled him and crawled on top, keeping their mouths together. His tongue was doing this intricate dance inside her mouth that made the hair on the back of her neck stand upright. She took her revenge by lowering her hips onto his groin. TJ countered with a move that slid both his hands up her torso to cup her breasts and suddenly she hated Wonderbra with a passion.

One motion stripped off her T-shirt. Another released her from the confining bra and TJ growled.

"Oh yes." He pulled her closer, catching hold of one nipple between his teeth. His fingers stroked her ribs, making her skin come alive as he sucked, switching from side to side. The slight breeze whispered past her wet nipples and they tightened even more. All around the gentle noises of nature carried on—birds chirping, the leaves rustling in an uneven beat. The slurps and moans and small cries of passion escaping their lips fit perfectly in the mix, and Pam thought she'd never been in a more beautiful place.

She pulled away to gaze at him, his ever-present smile warming her heart, the lust and passion on his face heating her soul. "As fun as this is, I don't think the roof is a good place to make love."

His eyes widened and he lunged upward to mesh their bodies together once more, and suddenly she found herself flat on her back under him. The blanket protected her from the ridges of the roof shingles and the sun broke out in full glory.

The light in his eyes outshone it.

"I think anywhere is a fabulous place to make love to you."

Her heart skipped a beat. Then she couldn't see his face anymore as he dropped toward her, his lips doing wicked things to her torso, his fingers playing her body as skillfully as he played his guitar. Oh yeah, he was talented. The simmer of desire in her belly bloomed, and oddly the roof of the cabin seemed a lovely place for a little sexual jaunt. Only...

"Did you bring a condom?" Even the question came out sounding like *fuck me now.* Breathless, needy. Lustful.

He rose over her. "We don't need one, you know. I won't carry any STDs since shifting to my wolf heals almost everything germ or virus related."

"Almost?"

The heavy weight of his groin pressed against her center as he nestled between her thighs, and it felt so good a little bit of her brain melted.

"The common cold still sucks."

Oh Lord, he kissed her again—kisses that were far too distracting. Far too enticing as he rocked their hips together intimately. The fabric separating them was a lifesaver and she wiggled under him. Sex was out unless they crawled off each other for long enough to gain the cabin. Still, there was no reason they couldn't still find satisfaction.

"Let me up."

He rolled off, disappointment written all over him. Until she stripped off her shorts and reached for his zipper.

"Are we going to...?"

"No." She manhandled him to his back and yanked off his pants. "We're not having sex without a condom. I'm sorry, what you said makes sense, but I can't just accept your word on something as big as that."

He lay back and threw an arm across his eyes, his chest heaving. His erection stood rampart straight from his groin. Hmm. The sexual hum in her body hit deafening levels so she reached out and grasped him firmly.

"Holy fuck." He thrust into her hand and she laughed.

"I'm no tease. We can go inside and grab a condom for round two. Right now..." Pam stroked him, her fingers passing lightly over the head of his erection to gather the moisture leaking from the tip. With her palm wet, it was easy to slide along his length, each pass drawing a groan of pleasure from his lips. The sunlight shone on them and she drew in a deep breath of the crisp air. The scent of their bodies rose around them and it made her happy inside.

Everything about TJ made her happy inside, if she was honest.

His hands grasped her hips and lifted her. "Shit, what the

hell are you doing?" She let go of his cock and threw out her hands to catch herself. A second later she was on hands and knees, palms resting on the blanket on either side of his hips. She followed the line of his body to where his head nestled between her knees. He licked his lips and her sex pulsed.

"You use your hands, but I get to use my mouth."

Yee-ha.

He tugged her backward and suddenly the fact they were on a roof vanished. The need to discover if they were mates? Out the proverbial window because the guy had a magical tongue and he was using it to her utmost advantage. He licked—light teasing touches, followed by full-out forceful sweeps from the sensitive skin near her anus to the apex of her mound.

Nibbles on her labia. Sucking her clit. She rocked back in an attempt to get him closer but his grip on her hips held her fast. He was in control and there was nothing she could do to change that fact.

Except distract him. She glanced at his cock and planned her counterattack. One hand on the roof to balance, one hand to wrap around him and pump.

The reverberation of his groan against her nether lips sent an electric shock racing. Fireworks zapped past her nipples and looped back to ignite the fuse in her core. He gripped her ass tighter, massaging and squeezing her cheeks as he ground her down on his face. His hot wet tongue slid into her, and it was so incredible she stopped moving for a second. Let the sensations build until she trembled on the verge of release. The euphoria took her so high that when he thrust two fingers deep into her core and sucked her clit hard, it was all over. Blood pounded past her ears and her head spun. It took a while until the waves slowed enough she could think again.

TJ lapped slowly, his touch more and more gentle until she let him help her shift to snuggle against his side. His turgid cock pressed her hip and she took a deep breath, guilt haunting her.

"Fuck, that was selfish of me."

TJ possessed her mouth for a long breathless kiss. The taste of her pleasure on his lips made her shiver.

He pulled away and touched their foreheads together. "Not selfish. Timing is everything. You needed to concentrate, and I wanted to give to you." He tugged her fingers to his lips and kissed her knuckles, and something in her heart tightened a little. What had he said about a physical connection? She rarely came from oral sex if she was giving at the same time.

Her finger was surrounded by wet heat as he sucked the digit into his mouth. One by one he wet them before placing her hand on his erection and wrapping his fingers over hers. "Now it's my turn, and you can give to me."

Tip to root he guided her, increasing the pressure. His lips found hers again, and their tongues slid together sensually as the stroke-stroke continued. Not too fast, but solid. Firm. Pam dug her fingers into his hair and tugged his head back, exposing his throat. He let her kiss her way down. She paused, breathing deeply with her face buried in his neck before licking back up, the salty taste of him like a fine wine. He filled her senses—the touch of their skin so wicked and sensual. The sound of their joint hands an erotic contrast with the delicate sounds of nature. He tightened under her hand and with a groan he came. The hot fluid of his ejaculation coated their hands and sprayed out farther to land willy-nilly between their naked torsos.

They sat together until their hearts stopped thumping, warmth radiating out from TJ like a space heater. Pam nestled closer and pressed their chests together, heedless of the semen on their skin.

"That was pretty awesome, if I do say so."

TJ grinned. "How about a shower before a little more awesome? I think we can work it into the schedule."

The schedule was getting better all the time. "Deal."

She grabbed their clothes into a pile and he protested mildly. "You want us to crawl down naked?"

Pam reached out a hand toward him, dragging a finger through the moisture clinging to his firm abdomen. "I'm not putting clothes on a sticky body for five minutes when they have to last us a week."

TJ shrugged, then picked up the blanket. She made her way cautiously to the edge of the roof and threw the clothes to the ground. TJ held her hand as she slipped a foot over to find the precarious top of the woodpile. Heading down wasn't as easy as she remembered the upward journey had been.

"I can't believe I actually raced up here."

Once both feet were down, one log wobbled underfoot and she grasped TJ firmer to regain her balance. She took her time, testing each step until she made it to the bottom safely. TJ copied her and threw down the blanket. He spun around to place his feet. *Hmm, what a nice ass.*

He descended a few steps and she was just thinking how nicely the front view complimented the back when a loud crack rang out. The logs under his feet rolled and bucked, and suddenly TJ was fast approaching the ground, almost surfing the pile of timber that had seemingly come to life. Individual logs shook and spun, some falling to the side, some twisting in place as the entire mound collapsed. The wood crackled and snapped with an alarming volume, the clatter echoing off the cabin wall. Random logs fell left and right as he twirled his arms to maintain balance. Pam stepped out of the path of danger, watching with dread as the stack disintegrated. The once neat load completed its tumble to the ground, one final log teetering for a second before joining the rest with a gentle *plop*, TJ askew on top of the messy heap.

Chapter Nine

TJ lay face down on the mattress, sure his face was as red as his butt. Stabbing pain shot through his right ass cheek, and he pressed up on his elbows with a curse.

"Damn it all, leave them. They'll fall out eventually. Ouch, shit. Stop it."

Pam laughed at him and applied the tweezers again, trying to remove a few more of the splinters he'd gained upon contact with the firewood. "Stop being such a whiny puppy."

He growled and her laughter grew louder. He collapsed and grit his teeth together. *Fuck,* it felt like she was digging post holes. "You having fun back there?"

"Uh-huh."

Shit. He cringed again at an especially hard spike. "Bet you sucked at playing Operation when you were little."

Pam gave an extra deep dig. "Horrible. Lost every time."

He buried his face in the pillow and bit it. Hard.

She giggled. An honest to God, full-out girlish giggle that ended in a snort and TJ couldn't take it anymore. He whirled, captured her in his arms and dragged her under him.

"Hey, I haven't got them all yet." She tangled her hands in his hair and pressed their mouths together, and all the splinters in the world weren't enough to distract him from finding a condom and pleasing his mate all over again.

And again. On the bed, in the shower. Heck, they barely got supper cooking before his wolf prompted him to press her to the tabletop and take her from behind. The fragrant aroma of tomato sauce filled the cabin, the water for the spaghetti noodles boiled unminded in the pot as he pounded into her. Pam's shouts of encouragement took them both to the edge quicker than he wanted. Every slide into her body nudged her farther into his heart. She reached back and grabbed his hand, threading their fingers together. He slowed and pressed his front to her back, twisting her head to the side to be able to stare into her eyes.

"This is real, Pam." He thrust forward slowly, gazes locked together. "You, me. Together like this."

She tightened her fingers.

Another rock of his hips. Another time being squeezed by her body so tight he could barely breathe. But it was the expression in her eyes that took his breath away.

So much hope, and so much fear. His wolf howled and he fought back the urge to claim her completely. Beat down the desire to take charge before she was ready. TJ closed his eyes and held on to control with a fine thread. All the while, they moved together.

It was probably the only thing that saved him. Pam's willing presses against him as she rose to meet his thrusts calmed his wolf. Gave him the chance to ease the beast back and return to his human control once more. He tucked one hand around her torso, one hand between her legs to help her along, rubbing her clit in time with their joining until he felt her tighten under him, her orgasm grasping him in waves. He buried himself in her and let his restraints go, wishing with all his heart she was ready to accept all of him.

Forever.

"Another list?"

TJ took another couple of slow paddles, directing their canoe toward the bay they had selected. Day four, and time was slipping away too rapidly. The afternoon sun sparkled around them, the setting as idyllic as any picture postcard, but he felt a sense of urgency he'd never had before in the wilderness. Proving they were mates was like proving to a child the sun would rise in the morning. Facts could only explain so much before you had to let go and trust. "You can put your paddle away and I'll let you take a peek. Oh, and you can turn around. I'm going to drop anchor while we fish."

Pam tucked away the paddle and carefully lifted her legs over the gunwales as she rotated. The long line of bare skin showing below the edge of her shorts made his mouth water, and he stared off into the bush and thought of nasty things to divert his mind.

When the canoe stopped rocking he checked to make sure she was seated comfortably, then passed over the papers he had stashed in his pocket. She unfolded them and smoothed the creases. "The mate list. Which one are we going to do today?"

"Complementary interests."

She stared at the paper and he wondered why she looked so sad. Why the burst of pleasure he felt from her faded so quickly to something close to despair. His connection with her had leveled out over the past two days, and he doubted it would grow any stronger until they actually made love without protection and he marked her as his. What they had now was like a shadow reflecting the real connection he considered

226

possible. It was there, undeniable to him, but he ached for more.

Pam put on a happy face and refolded the paper, tucking it into her back pocket. She glanced at the second sheet of paper still lying in her lap and laughed. "Oh my God, are you expecting me to write an essay or something? I'm on holidays. I'm not into reports right now."

"Hell no, those are topics to discuss. See, most mates I know have common interests. Robyn and Keil, you should see them on the slopes. They're both totally insane skiers when they're not leading a group. Erik and Maggie are both classical literature buffs."

"So you think we should have a bunch of interests in common?"

She settled into the bottom of the canoe and adjusted her lifejacket so she could lean back on the front seat and use it as a backrest. Her long legs stretched out into the center of the craft, and TJ eyed them with longing. He sighed. No. While he'd been more fortunate than usual with his clumsiness so far this week, fooling around in a canoe would not end up a pretty picture.

"TJ?"

He caught her eye and stumbled for words. "I was staring again, wasn't I?"

She blushed lightly, then tossed her head back, her dark hair bouncing around her shoulders. "I don't mind. But back to the question..."

"I think we could have things in common, or we could be like Tad and Missy—they often have interests that when you put them together you get something that fits. He makes things out of wood and she enjoys sewing. Together they've made all kinds of gifts for the pack, like baby cradles and receiving blankets, and decorative wall quilts and hangers to display them on."

Pam nodded slowly. "They complete each other. You think we're going to have matches like that?"

"Over the past couple days as we've talked I think I've heard a few things, but I don't want to skew the results and use those as an example. So you pick one item, think of an answer but before you tell me what you would say, I'll share mine."

She grinned as she examined the paper. "This could be fun you know."

Her mischief-maker persona was back. God, he loved it when her eyes got all sparkly and her face lit up. It made it easier to breath. Made the whole of his soul content.

He baited the hooks, added a bobber and cast out the line, passing the first rod to her before setting up his own. Fishing was a great opportunity for long conversations.

Pam ran a finger down the list before glancing at him, an innocent expression plastered to her face. *Not.* "Okay—what's your favourite sport for exercise?"

Easy. "Running." Mostly as a wolf, but that still counted.

She snorted. "Mine is baseball. Well, that one works, we can play fetch together, right?"

He flicked water at her and the boat rocked lightly as she laughed.

"Number two. Favourite thing to do to relax?"

TJ gripped the fishing rod firmly in lieu of reaching for her. "My new response would be to make love with you, but before this week I would have said make music."

The flash of desire in her eyes was unmistakable. "Stop."

They stared at each other. Her pulse pounded in the hollow of her throat and he ached. "What's your answer, Pam?"

She licked her lips. "I was going to say listen to music."

Yup, she could try to deny it, but there was more and more evidence to prove they were meant to be together.

Her fishing rod quivered and she scrambled upright, the paper falling unminded to the bottom of the canoe. He laughingly coached her through reeling in the fish. For the next two hours they floated and fished, releasing all but one of the rainbow trout while they worked their way through the entire list he'd prepared. By now the paper was wet and smelled like fish, and when the time came to turn the canoe back toward the dock Pam had nothing but content emotions streaming from her.

"You relax, I'll get us home." He paddled hard, eyes on the water occasionally. Most of the time his gaze caressed her body where she leaned back, arms resting easily on the gunwales as she glanced around at the nearby mountains.

"I can't believe someone gets to live here for more than a holiday."

"The summers are fabulous, but in a remote location like this they don't stay all winter, and winter comes early in the North. My friends usually use this cabin from May to August, then they have a place farther south for the rest of the year."

He stroked evenly, wondering why it was far harder than usual to keep the canoe headed in a straight line. It was too clichéd to think looking at her made him weak with desire.

"When does the helicopter return for us?" Her eyes were closed as she spoke, the lazy contentment still emanating from her. TJ relaxed from the instant alert her question had raised.

"Around two o'clock, three days from now. We'll get dropped off in Haines, and we'll have to get a lift back to Maggie and Erik's. The tour you were supposed to take will be done by noon."

She laughed and leaned forward to wrap her arms around her knees. Her dark eyes sparkled at him. "Thank you."

"For what?"

Pam pointed around. "For this. I know we've still got unanswered questions between the two of us, but I wouldn't give up this experience for anything. I like this much better, being quiet and remote. It's far more my style than the daily routine of traveling with a tour group."

TJ stuttered for a second in confusion. "You signed up for it. That first day you said I had no right—"

She raised a hand. "I know, I was wrong. I went along with Maggie's suggestion because I didn't see any other possible way to experience the wilderness in a short time. A single female, traveling alone, just isn't smart. You did okay when you kidnapped me. You really did know a little bit about what I truly needed."

"Well, I'm glad you're comfortable with it now."

Her soft smile teased him. "You're comfortable—in a completely unsettling and life-unraveling way."

They laughed together easily and TJ drew in a deep breath of the crisp air. Hope stirred.

He switched paddling sides to give his arm a rest. They were closing in on the dock but he'd never found a canoe to be so awkward and slow to maneuver.

Pam trailed her fingers in the water lazily, ribbons of waves streaming out on either side of her fingers. Three days left to make a difference. TJ wondered briefly what chaos was happening back in Haines, but he'd pay that piper when he had to. Now they had a rainbow trout to enjoy for supper, and the evening stretched open before them.

From the expression in her eyes she had a few ideas of how

they could spend their time, and he'd be a willing participant in anything she planned.

They arrived at the dock and he held firm to the decking as she scrambled out. All the equipment came out one at a time until he looked around for the anchor.

Pam burst out laughing, gesturing behind the canoe. "Are those greens to accompany the fish for dinner?"

He swung his head to see a huge mess of lake weed gathered behind the boat. "Where did that come from?" He scrambled onto the dock and followed the line of her pointing finger. "Oh shit. No wonder it was so hard to paddle."

Pam lay on her belly on the deck to grab the anchor rope. She pulled, hauling up the weeds and the anchor he'd neglected to bring in, instead trailing it behind them the whole length of the lake.

He sighed. Yup, two steps forward, one step back. At least it was better than tipping them over.

TJ sat on the steps of the porch, plucking the strings of the old guitar they'd found in the storage closet. Every day since she'd discovered he was a wolf, he'd played for her. She'd grown to anticipate the quiet time to sit and think. Today more than ever she needed it. Tomorrow would be their last full day together before the helicopter returned. Pam curled up on the porch swing and watched the sunset. They faced the lake straight on, and the glow rising behind the western mountains painted the entire scene in shades of tangerine and gold. Streaks of light shone on them, and she smiled when TJ's dark colouring lightened as a brilliant flash of pink lit his torso.

The gentle tones of the guitar washed over her. She closed her eyes and rocked dreamily, reveling in her situation. A full belly, a glass of wine at her elbow. After-dinner music. Life couldn't get much better.

She had slight aches and pains from the various activities of the past days. True to his word, TJ had let her try out all kinds of outdoor experiences, including a madcap kayak trip down the nearby river.

Also true to his word, some of her aches were from the very frequent and extremely pleasurable hot wolfie sex they'd been enjoying. And for the past day, every time he grabbed a condom from their dwindling supply she'd been close to telling him to forget it...

It was official. She was going mad.

The kidnapping was no longer an issue. They had become good enough friends it was actually kind of difficult to remember this wasn't what she'd signed up for. She had questions that remained, but her lurking suspicion was when the week officially came to an end, she would be reluctant to leave him behind and head south to resume her normal routine.

The change in her mental processes bewildered her.

"That was a big sigh." TJ examined her closely, his dark eyes peering into her soul. "What deep thoughts are making you so sad?"

Shit. The relaxed peace faded a little. There was such a short time left before their ride appeared to return them to civilization, and she still didn't know what to do. "Thinking about everything you've shown me. You know, the mating list and all."

He strummed softly for a minute, the light melody from the finger-picked strings floating around them. He meant to soothe her, she was sure of it, but as the now-familiar tune he played filled her ears and her heart, tears threatened. It was the same song he'd sung to her at the wedding, with eternal love and new hope all tied up in it.

She wanted more and more to believe.

TJ leaned back on the upper porch railing. "There's this older couple who run the Chilkat Bakery in town. Both human. I think they said they've been married for fifty-five years."

Pam glanced at him with suspicion. Where was this going? "So?"

He placed the guitar aside and joined her on the swing. "You ever seen a couple like that? Married for so long, they seem to read each other's minds?" He wrapped a hand around her neck to massage the tight muscles. "They seem to know exactly what the other person needs at any time."

"Are you saying humans can have a mating connection? I've never heard that before in my life."

"Okay, maybe it's not exactly the same thing, but it must be fairly close. I've seen it. They know each other so deeply they anticipate each other's thoughts, and needs. That's what it's like for wolves—the only thing that seems to be different is how quickly it happens. For wolves, it's instant. In humans, I've seen it in couples who have been together for a long time."

Pam bit her lip. *Frick.* Again, him with the logic. She couldn't fight logic, and yet the ball of fear in her belly didn't want to disappear.

"What are your parents like?"

She turned toward him. Yeah, he knew all the right buttons to push, far better than any person she'd met before. Not even Maggie had asked about her family that quickly. "We're divorced."

TJ's face fell. "Shit."

"Yeah."

"Okay, so I guess they're not a great example." He stopped and stared at her for second. "Hang on, what do you mean 'we're divorced'?"

Pam dragged a hand through her hair. "They got divorced when I was about ten, and proceeded to make my life miserable. They both screwed up holiday plans to get revenge on the other. They fought over me like a dog with a bone, but when they had time with me they ignored me, or seemed to begrudge the fact they had to expend energy on my stuff."

"By the time I was sixteen I'd had enough. I divorced them and went to live with my gramma who was completely disgusted with them both. She passed away when I was nineteen. I've been on my own ever since."

She said it simply, a statement of fact. Taking control of her life ten years ago at such a young age had been hard, but she'd had to do it. It had been the right thing, she was sure.

TJ kissed her temple softly, then nestled her under his arm. He linked their fingers together and rested their joined hands in his lap. "Do you ever see your parents?"

She shook her head. "And it's not because I'm hiding from them. Honestly, I'm not bitter or wishing them ill anymore. I cut the ties and decided I was responsible for my own happiness. They just don't seem to give a damn. I think I remind them of each other or something, and they hate each other with a vengeance." She shrugged.

He grimaced. "So telling you stories about human happily-ever-afters..."

Pam leaned back on him and sighed. "Sheer fantasy. Werewolves are a whole lot more believable." A whole lot more desirable as well, from what she could tell. TJ appeared to know exactly who he was and where he stood. Had he gained that confidence from being a wolf?

TJ stroked her fingers gently with his thumb. "I've had the pack around me all my life. While I get razzed a great deal for being clumsy, they've always supported me. My brother, my friends, heck...everyone."

"You're not clumsy."

He laughed out loud. "Okay, there's another topic for discussion. Umm, yes, I am. For some reason I'm not nearly as bad when I'm around you." He nuzzled her neck. "That 'you complete me' thing."

She slapped him lightly. "Get out. I think you're like a puppy coming into his growth. You should have seen the trouble my first dog had—"

He groaned. "Can we make a deal now that you don't compare me to your previous dogs. Please?"

A snort slipped out. "We'll see."

She twisted to stare at him. His earnest expression stole her heart.

"Pam, can you give me a clue here? Have I persuaded you at all what I said is true? That we're mates?"

Her fears and doubts scrambled to stay above the undeniable bond between them that grew stronger every moment she spent with him.

"Can't you tell what I'm thinking with that wolf connection of yours?" She couldn't speak over a whisper, the effort of pushing the words out enormous. She wanted to believe, wanted it so very much.

He surprised her by lifting her into his lap and tucking her head against his chest before setting the porch swing rocking. He surrounded her with his arms as if pulling a shield of protection around them. "I sense all kinds of things from you, and yet your emotions are so jumbled I can't understand. Fear, longing, sexual need. At times I feel as if you're about to announce you love me. The next minute you're planning to tell me goodbye and expect I'll drop you at the airport and let you go without a word of protest."

Umm, yup, that would about cover the gamut of chaos running through her brain the past couple days.

"Do you really pick up all those things, or are you guessing?"

It was his turn to sigh. "I can't literally read your mind, and we can't speak to each other mentally. But as far as I can tell, I'm just about as linked to you in terms of a mate connection as I could dream of."

"I feel like I've known you all my life." The whispered confession eased the tightness inside a little. He squeezed her gently and kissed the top of her head. His heart thumped solidly under her ear, and she snuck her arms around his torso to draw as close as possible.

TJ sang to her *a capella*, his rich voice tickling her ears. Filling her with hope and a deep longing.

My love will never fade, it lingers like the light.
Fills all the mountaintops, burning ever bright.
My love is like the tide, fresh and clean each day.
It's pure and strong, and all that I can say—
You fill my days, you fill my nights, you're everything, all I need,
Forever

My love is like the spring, it lingers like the snow.
It only melts away, to bring new growth.

My love is like the wind, running wild and free.

Together now, won't you come with me—

You fill my days, you fill my nights, you're everything, all I need,

Forever

He let the words trail off, the intensity of his song wrapped up with all the things she felt from him. His tender heart. His humour. Plain spoken and blunt, but never cruel, he was all the things she admired in a friend. All the things she wanted in a lover.

Her final doubts dissolved. Logic had a place in this, and he'd done his best to show her the mate list existed and examples of each item. But at some point, the heart had to take over from the head and that moment was now.

She pressed her palm against his cheek and kissed him softly before crawling off his lap and holding out her hand.

"What—?"

She shook her head. One finger held to her lips, she poured her energy into sharing what she felt inside. The deep satisfaction at his company. The passion she held for him.

The love.

They walked together, hand in hand, into the cabin where she led him to the bedroom. She stripped off her clothes quickly and turned to help him. With every touch of her hands, she thought of a moment he'd made her smile the past week. Of an expression she'd seen on his face. Of the love she'd seen in his eyes. She didn't need any more words—he'd been saying it to her all week long with every gesture, every touch.

Every time he'd shifted into his wolf and wandered at her side, or curled up against her, soft and warm. He was completely comfortable in both his skins, and there was no deceit in him.

She tugged him to the bed and they connected, skin on skin, hands brushing, exploring. Their lips met in a breathless kiss that began soft and gentle before turning ravenous. Greedy and passionate, they rolled together until she managed to maneuver into position, his legs trapped under her. His cock breached the folds of her body and they slid together in one perfect moment. His breath released with a gasp and she felt his muscles tense as he realized they were making love without any barrier between them.

TJ gathered her in his arms and peered into her eyes. He didn't ask if she was sure, didn't do anything to break the beauty of her gift. He didn't even speak, not with words.

But his eyes said *I love you.*

His body said it. So did all the emotion she sensed from him, whether a figment of her imagination or not. All signs said he was hers, completely.

They moved together, hips rocking, tension building. The aching need to be filled by him, not only physically, but in every way, being answered. Kisses upon kisses fell while TJ's hands roamed her body. He slid into her again and again, drawing her thigh high over his hip as they lay side by side on the mattress. She teetered on the edge of release. He buried his face in her neck, rising slightly to press deeper into her core, the angle change pressing harder against her clit. The tickly sensation preceding her climax had never built this high before and every nerve screamed for satisfaction. She had no idea how intense her body's response would be when he put his teeth to her neck and bit down, burying himself deep as they both went off together.

Bright white pleasure raced over her, every bit of skin

sensitive and tingling. Every breath of air tasted like him, every thought wrapped up in his love. Their bodies meshed, intimate and close, as waves of bliss pulsed repetitively. The bundle of dreams she'd tied up and put aside as impossible unwound.

Forever was not a myth, no more than werewolves.

They lay tangled together for the longest time, their breathing slowly returning to normal. TJ kissed her—her neck, her cheek, her forehead. One soft lingering kiss to her mouth. He spoke, their lips brushing together.

"I can feel your heart in my soul."

Chapter Ten

TJ closed the door to the cabin with reluctance. Neither of them was ready to leave. He turned to see Pam grinning at him, her pack already on her back as they prepared to meet the helicopter. It still seemed impossible she'd taken that final step and accepted him. One day to celebrate being fully mated—it wasn't enough.

"I should have taken a two-week excursion. Then we could have stayed for another week."

She held out her hand and he joined her, strolling to the meadow with their fingers linked together. TJ lifted her fingers to his mouth and kissed her knuckles lightly. "While I'd love more time alone, at some point we need to face the real world."

Oh hell, and there would be some facing to do. Funny though, now that he and Pam were fully mated, he wasn't nearly as worried to see what the fallout from his actions would be. They truly were together—there was no denying it—and no one could tear them apart. They dropped their packs at the side of the clearing and Pam returned to his arms, resting her head on his chest. She drew a deep breath. "Can we come back here sometime?"

"Definitely."

He played with her hair as they silently stood together. Ever since they'd completed their mating, he had a solid line on what she was feeling. Compared to how it had been before, the richness and depth was incredible. Like having watched an old-fashioned black-and-white movie on a five-inch screen and now getting Blu-ray, hi-def flashing across a wall-sized monitor.

Right now she was content, and he was going to do everything he could to keep her that way.

"You know we've got a bunch of 'meet the family' to do, right?" he warned her.

Pam lifted her arms to drape them around his neck. "I think I can handle it. Maggie and Erik won't be back yet, but I'm not afraid to meet your brother, or his wife, more formally. Or anyone else I need to see."

TJ kissed her, unable to resist one more dose of her taste to bolster him. It was going to be an interesting day, if nothing else.

The sound of the chopper reached them long before they spotted it in the distance, and she clung to him for a second, squeezing him tight. "I know we've got a ton to figure out, but, honestly? It'll all work out. I'm sure it will."

"Of course it will." Her faith became his faith, and together, there was nothing they couldn't do.

Shaun landed, his grinning face peering out the window. They tossed their packs into the passenger area and scrambled after them, strapping themselves in and quickly donning headsets. They lifted off and Pam hung over him to gaze back at the cabin and lake as they swung around to return to Haines. Her body was warm and soft against him, and he wrapped an arm around her to keep her close.

"Well, I don't have to ask if you had a good time." Shaun's voice cut in over the headset. "Congratulations, both of you."

Pam glanced at TJ in surprise. He pressed the talk button to explain. "The wolf sense of smell. Shaun can tell we're mates."

"He can tell…" She flushed. "Okay, maybe I'm not so ready to meet your pack as I thought."

TJ grabbed her hand and squeezed.

Shaun spoke again. "I need to give you the scoop. I managed to stay off your big brother's radar for the past week, but I got a direct order from my Alpha in Whitehorse to report to him as soon as I get you two home safe. Which is fine, since that means I won't have to face Keil."

TJ swore. "I didn't intend to get you in trouble when I asked for help."

"Hey, no worries. You would have done the same thing for me if you could. You're a good friend, TJ, and it's nice to have been able to assist you two lovebirds. I don't think my Alpha will give me shit—he's a romantic at heart. Makes us watch bad chick flicks during pack meetings, yada yada."

"Still, let me know if you need me to come and talk to your Alpha. I have a feeling I'll be explaining myself constantly for the next while."

Shaun held a thumbs-up. "Anyway, I contacted your pack via email to let them know I'd drop you at the airstrip. Someone should be there to pick you up. I'm afraid you're on your own after that."

Pam's hand in his was all the reminder he needed. "I'm never going to be alone again."

She leaned against him and used the headset. "So, the shit is about to hit the fan, is it?"

"Don't know why it should. You're not going to call the cops and have me arrested, right?"

"I am the cops."

They grinned at each other.

A beige minivan stood at the side of the airstrip—Tad and Missy's vehicle—and TJ breathed a sigh of relief. The pack Omegas would be the perfect people to talk to first. TJ passed down the packs to Pam then squeezed Shaun on the shoulder. "Thanks again for everything."

"Hey, give me a second." Shaun twisted in his seat to face TJ. "You know what? I think they're going to be very surprised when they meet you, your brother and the rest of them. You've changed. Something happened to you and you're more than the wolf I dropped off a week ago."

TJ frowned. "What do you mean?"

Shaun shook his head. "Not sure, but let's put it this way, I doubt I could order you to do anything for me anymore."

Fuck. "Really?"

"Really." Shaun winked at him and turned back to his instrument panel. "Now get out of here, your mate is waiting for you."

TJ joined Pam on the tarmac and they shouldered their packs, heading toward the van. TJ's mind spun. Shaun couldn't order him around? Shaun had always outranked him—heck most wolves seemed to outrank him. Not that they made a big deal of it, but usually he was "the younger brother of the Alpha" and otherwise not very interesting to most of the pack.

Tad stepped from the van and popped the hatch. Then he stood back and looked them up and down while they piled their backpacks into the vehicle. His wry smile was somewhat reassuring.

"Welcome back. And welcome to the pack, Pam. Congratulations on your mating."

Pam tugged on TJ's sleeve. "Everyone knows on sight we're mates. This is going to take some serious getting used to."

TJ opened the passenger door for her and helped her in. "I said there were things that were hard to explain—you kind of have to experience them to understand." He scooted into the backseat.

She turned to answer Tad who had crawled behind the wheel. "Thanks. You'll have to warn me if I do something wrong. You're the pack...Omega, right?"

Tad nodded. "TJ explained a little about how wolves operate?"

"Yeah, he explained a lot. That doesn't mean much until I see it in motion. Bottom line, I didn't plan on joining any country clubs, I just..."

"We just want to be together." TJ eased forward between the seats, laying a hand on Pam's arm.

"Well, together is great and all that, but I hope you're ready to face the music. Robyn's been walking around all week like a thunderstorm ready to happen, and Keil got back half an hour ago and he's brewing up a storm as well. Missy is trying to settle them both down before we arrive, but we'll see how well it works."

"They'll have to get over it." The words were braver spoken than the pit in his stomach acknowledged. Pam glanced over her shoulder and a breeze-like sensation brushed him. She pictured them sitting together, him making music, her admiring the scenery. She gave her calm to him and he pulled her fingers to his lips. He kissed them softly then whispered, "Cool trick."

She grinned. "I think I'm getting the hang of this."

Tad hmmed. "This is very interesting. I can read you, TJ, like I normally can, but Pam—it's like she's wolf and yet not. I had no idea you were able to share emotions in a mating between humans and wolves."

"But you haven't been a full wolf for long, have you?" Pam asked.

"No. Still, at the core what I do sense from you two is that you belong together, and you're good for each other. But that's my interpretation, and it's not my place to make decisions about your life for you."

"Damn straight," Pam muttered.

TJ laughed. "Speak up now, Pam, tell us how you really feel."

Tad smiled. "So, what *have* you decided?"

She dragged aside the collar of her T-shirt to reveal the mark TJ had left when he bit her. The wound had healed way faster than they'd expected—some kind of wolfie magic.

Tad nodded. "Well, that's pretty cut and dried. You know, it's kind of interesting not being able to read you the same way I can read the rest of the pack. I think you're going to be good for us all."

He turned down the long, narrow driveway that led to the cluster of homes built against the trees on the outskirts of Haines. He pulled up in front of an older log house, a wide veranda running the length of the building. TJ scrambled out to join Pam. A tricycle with pink streamers sat in the middle of the walkway, and Tad pushed it to the side as they approached the front doors.

TJ grasped Pam's hand in his, locking fingers.

"I feel like we should be offered a last meal or something." Pam hummed part of the funeral dirge and TJ laughed.

Tad frowned at them. "What song was that?"

Pam rolled her eyes and glared at TJ. "See, I told you I couldn't sing. So much for your lessons that night at the cabin."

TJ shrugged. "I'm your mate, I'm not a miracle worker."

She growled and swung at him. He caught the blow and pulled her against him, capturing her lips. She tasted like sunshine and sex, and if he didn't need to go see what Keil and Robyn had planned as retribution, he would pick her up and go hide in the woods for a few hours.

Or a few days. He was easy.

She kissed him back, her fingers lacing through his hair. He loved the way her tongue took control, exploring and teasing until all his body heard the wake-up call. She moved closer, her soft skin and strong muscles matching him perfectly. Especially when he reached down and cupped her butt, dragging her tighter against him and—

"TJ, Pam. So glad you could drop in." Keil's deep voice cut through the sexual fog and they wrenched apart. His brother spun on his heel and entered the house, leaving the door open behind him.

Pam's cheeks were flushed, but she lifted her chin high and stepped forward by his side.

"He's not really a jerk. I mean, sometimes he is, but usually he's a pretty good guy. Really." Although it appeared this might be one of the "jerk" days.

Pam snorted. "Don't worry about me, I have a feeling it's your ass he wants in a sling."

TJ nodded slowly. "Well, there is that."

They entered the main room and TJ counted heads. Keil and Robyn, Tad and Missy. A number of other high-level wolves were in attendance, but on the whole it seemed like a pretty friendly gathering.

Well, friendly except for Robyn, who gave him the evil eye as she leaned against the far wall. Keil stood at the foot of the staircase, arms crossed in front of his chest like a freaking bulldozer, ready to crush him underfoot.

Complete confidence held TJ up. Beside him stood his mate, her amusement at the situation flowing to him and calming his concerns. Heck, if she wasn't worried, why should he be? These were his family and friends. There was nothing they would do to him that wasn't done out of love.

"Umm, hi, everyone. You all met Pam at the wedding, but I'd like to introduce her again. It's official, she's accepted me as her mate."

Like that was a surprise to anyone with a nose, but he figured for Pam's sake he should say it, before some wiseass decided to ask how in the world they had managed to get as sex-scented as they were. It wasn't his fault they took that final shower together. It had been all her idea.

Keil moved closer, towering over him.

"Don't you ever pull such a harebrained stunt again. What the hell were you thinking?" he roared.

TJ opened his mouth to respond when Pam stepped between them. She pasted her fists on her hips and glared up at Keil. "Don't you shout at him. He's already apologized to me and I'm the only one he needs to worry about."

Holy shit. Keil's jaw nearly hit the floor. Off to the side Tad stared at the ceiling, biting his lip. TJ watched closely and he would have sworn Tad was laughing.

Keil cleared his throat and glanced around the room sheepishly. When he spoke again, he turned down the volume and spoke more respectfully. "I'm sorry, you're right. There's no need for me to raise my voice. I'm not talking about you and him right now. I'm talking about him not leaving word of where he had arranged to take you, or having a backup plan to contact help if you got in trouble. He knows that's not proper procedure in terms of safety in the wilderness."

Pam nodded slowly. "Oh. I thought you were going to give him grief for kidnapping me. By all means, if he screwed up protocol—ream him out." She stepped back and gestured with a hand. The room broke out with laughter.

Keil raised a brow. "So kind of you to give me permission."

TJ scratched his face to hide his own smile. Yup, this was going to work out fine, once he took his lumps, because Keil was right about the safety issues.

Keil hauled a cell phone out of his pocket and slapped it into TJ's palm. "You'll probably need this—I found it back at base camp after you took off. Oh, and did you even try the satellite phone you took with you? The batteries on that one were nearly dead."

A solid smack landed on his arm as Pam hit him. "Dead? What if I'd wanted to call for the chopper?"

"But you broke..." TJ buttoned his lip. There was no way he was even going to touch this one.

Pam growled at him, her eyes flashing. "Next time, let me do the trip planning."

TJ tried to hide his smile. "Of course."

"Holy crap, she's the most alpha human I've ever met," one of the observer wolves piped up.

Pam frowned. "Alpha? Isn't that your position?" she asked Keil.

He shook his head. "Yes and no. Alpha isn't just about leadership, it also refers to how strong you are, mentally as well as physically. There's more than one alpha wolf in any pack. Heck, Erik and Maggie, the pack Betas, are as strong as Robyn and I, but they've chosen to use their strengths in a different way. We can't all be bad-asses, you know."

"So there's no trouble with us being together?" Pam returned to TJ's side.

Keil shrugged. "There are a few old-timers in the pack who are whining about how the world is going to hell in a hand basket, but it's nothing I can't take care of."

Robyn clapped her hands and Keil pulled a face. "Oh yeah, and Robyn plans on having a long talk with your mate about some advice she gave that he ignored."

Oh shit. Okay, that was scarier than getting called on the carpet by Keil. TJ waved at Robyn tentatively and she flipped him the bird.

Pam grinned at TJ. "You know how I said I wasn't sure about dealing with your pack? No problem, I got it figured it. This is like hanging out at headquarters with the boys."

Tad stepped forward and gestured to the couch. "If you'd like to relax, I think the formal hazing is over. I do have one last question I'm curious about, and maybe someone with more experience can answer. What's up with TJ's strength? I'd swear he's gotten stronger since he left."

"Shaun said the same thing. What the hell are you talking about? I don't feel any different." TJ sat next to Pam. She kicked off her shoes and curled up almost in his lap. She tucked a hand under his arm and tickled his ribs lightly. "The only thing I know is I don't seem to be nearly as clumsy anymore. Well, relatively speaking."

Tad's mate, Missy, paced the floor to sit on the second couch across from them, one of her two-month-old babies cuddled against her shoulder. "Your wolf never has been clumsy."

Pam leaned forward. "I think his wolf is more grown up. Matured a bit. If TJ is twenty-two, that means his wolf is…" She turned to face him and asked, "What are wolf years, seven like dogs?"

He groaned. "You promised you wouldn't do that anymore."

Pam smirked at him. "If you're gonna play with the big dogs, you use every tool you can."

He opened his mouth to protest and suddenly the cell phone Keil had returned to him rang. Some joker had reprogrammed the phone tones to "Who Let the Dogs Out" and Pam cracked up.

He stood to answer it, leaving Pam and Missy giggling together furiously.

"Hello?"

"You idiot. You couldn't wait until we were done our honeymoon? Sheesh."

"Hi, Maggie." TJ took a deep breath. So much for him being stronger. There was no way he could get a word in edgewise with all these women around. He listened to her scolding for a minute before he had the most brilliant idea. "Hey, Maggie. I bet you need to talk to Pam. She's right here."

He held out the phone to his mate and she took it with surprise. Her surprise turned to delight and she rose to find a quieter spot to chat with her best friend.

TJ glanced around the room. Missy rocked one baby in her arms while Tad paced with her twin sister. Robyn was holding a conversation with someone, her hands moving rapidly.

Kara, Keil and Robyn's two-year-old daughter, crossed the room to Pam's side. She tugged on Pam's pant leg then reached her arms up. Pam leaned over and picked up the little girl who immediately wrapped herself close, her face buried in Pam's neck. Pam resumed her phone conversation.

Deep satisfaction filled TJ as everywhere he looked he saw family. Sharing together, laughing together. Little Jamie, Missy and Tad's oldest child, rolled on the floor with a couple of the pack in their wolf forms.

It wasn't the Waltons but it was home.

He glanced back at Pam to find her staring at him, a burning light in her eyes. She adjusted the girl in her arms and waggled her brows, tilting her head toward the child.

Oh shit. Oh shit, yeah. Well, maybe not this minute, but...

TJ winked at her and she grinned, blowing him a kiss.

Keil poked him in the shoulder. "You haven't heard a word I've said, have you? What's that goofy expression for?"

TJ took a deep breath. His head filled with the familiar scents of home, and overlaying it all was Pam. In his head, and his heart.

Forever.

"It's because I'm finally in the right place, at the right time. Excuse me, I'll be back for my lickings regarding safety, because you're right, I screwed up. And I'll apologize to Robyn in a minute as well. But there's something I need to do with my mate."

He stepped across the room and tugged Pam into the kitchen, taking little Kara along for the ride since she refused to let go of her newfound friend. He held out his hand for the phone.

"Mags? I gotta go. I think TJ wants me to take him for a walk."

TJ rubbed his forehead as she said goodbye to Maggie. A dog handler. She must have a million jokes all lined up and ready to spring on him.

Pam handed back his cell and batted her eyes. "Well. I thought that all went marvelously."

He groaned. "Yeah, I can see this relationship is going to

251

keep me on my toes. I wanted to know if you still had the mate list."

Pam frowned. "It's in my pocket. Why?"

"I never got to finish it."

She kissed Kara on the forehead then passed her to TJ. The little girl squirmed to be put down, returning with a laugh to the main room.

Pam reached into her back pocket and unfolded the paper on the counter. The edges were a little more tattered and ragged than when they started less than a week ago. She cupped his face in her hands. "You proved enough for me to take a chance, and while we've still got stuff to figure out, I think we're on our way."

TJ grabbed a pen. "I agree, but there's something I need you to see. It's important."

There where the five circles overlapped, an empty space remained. He'd deliberately made sure it was a part of every single circle and with great care he filled in one word.

Forever.

Pam sucked in air and threw her arms around his neck. He stumbled for a second to catch his balance as she crawled up him and kissed him madly. Oh yes, she was going to fit in fine. A room full of people on the other side of the wall and she was happily attempting to touch his tonsils.

He clasped her under the hips and turned to carry her to one of the back guestrooms. No one would notice if they were MIA for an hour or so, would they?

"Stop."

Shit. Please don't get all human shy. "They're all wolves. They wouldn't care if we had sex in the room in front of them."

Pam snorted. "Yeah, well, I doubt I'll ever get to that stage of comfort, but just let me get..." She leaned over and snatched the mate list off the counter. "Okay, now we can go fool around."

TJ laughed as he headed down the hall. "You going to keep that list?"

"Uh-huh. Just like you wrote. I'm planning on keeping it, and you, forever."

About the Author

Vivian Arend has hiked, biked, skied and paddled her way around most of North America and parts of Europe. Throughout all the wandering in the wilderness, stories have been planted and they are bursting out in vivid colour. Paranormal, twisted fairytales, red-hot contemporaries—the genres are all over.

Between times of living with no running water, she home schools her teenaged children and tries to keep up with her husband—the instigator of most of the wilderness adventures.

She loves to hear from readers: vivarend@gmail.com. You can also drop by http://vivianarend.com for more information on what is coming next.

They've been hiding from the past.
Now it's time to fight for their future.

Sanctuary Unbound
© *2010 Moira Rogers*

New England is ideal for vampire Adam Dubois. His cozy home in the Great North Woods reminds him of a happier time when werewolves and witches were stuff of legends, and he was a simple lumberjack.

Hiding from past failures has worked for over eighty years, but a life debt owed to the Red Rock alpha has forced him to leave his retreat—and come face to face with a woman who challenges and tempts him on every level.

Hiding secrets is a lonely business, and Cindy Shepherd is lonely with a capital L. Red Rock isn't exactly crawling with available men, but her interest in the mystery-shrouded new vampire in town seems mutual. After all, it's only sex—there's no danger he'll dig deep enough to unleash the demons of her past.

Casual flirtation turns deadly serious when Adam discovers that the vampire plaguing Red Rock is using his mistakes as a road map. When it comes to his life, he knows Cindy has his back. But in order to secure the future, they both must trust each other with more—even if it means sacrificing themselves to save everything they hold dear.

Warning: This book contains epic werewolf battles, mystical vampire blood bonds, unexpected sex on the kitchen floor and a dangerous attraction between a secret-burdened werewolf and a vampire lumberjack.

Available now in ebook and print from Samhain Publishing.

CPSIA information can be obtained at www.ICGtesting.com
Printed in the USA
LVOW12s1531030414

380211LV00002B/345/P